DATE			

BOBBIE LOUISE HAWKINS

MY OWN
ALPHABET

STORIES, ESSAYS & MEMOIRS

COFFEE HOUSE PRESS :: MINNEAPOLIS :: 1989

The publisher thanks the following organizations whose sup-
port helped make this book possible: The National Endowment
for the Arts, a federal agency; General Mills; and United Arts.

Coffee House Press books are distributed to trade by Consor-
tium Book Sales and Distribution, 213 East Fourth Street, Saint
Paul, Minnesota 55101. Our books are also available through all
major library distributors and jobbers, and through most small
press distributors, including Bookpeople, Bookslinger, Inland,
Pacific Pipeline, and Small Press Distribution. For personal
orders, catalogs or other information, write to:
COFFEE HOUSE PRESS
27 NORTH FOURTH STREET, SUITE 400
MINNEAPOLIS, MINNESOTA 55401.

Library of Congress Cataloging in Publication Data

Hawkins, Bobbie Louise, 1930 –
    My own alphabet : stories, essays & memoirs / by Bobbie
Louise Hawkins.
        p. cm.
    ISBN 0-918273-52-8 : $9.95
    I. Title
PS3553.R34M9   1989
818'.5409 – dc20   89-7354
                                CIP

Contents

* A *

Abortion

Dr. Gore was an abortionist. Hearts broke before his eyes. Young women sat in his office with their faces blanked as they thought of their altered future. Given that face and the mother who had learned about him from a friend who was a nurse and who didn't know whether he would help but who knew he was all she had, he was an abortionist.

Contempt and blame was the commonplace response to knocked-up girls in 1948 boondocks America. I expected it. I was ashamed. I had been a fool and I had been caught. He ignored my mother, who sat crying. It wasn't her fault—it was mine, and he despised me for it.

He rode a dangerous edge. Every time he agreed to save this latest mess, he put himself and his own future in the balance. All those girls and women left bleeding and butchered by the clothes-hanger brigade made him someone for the authorities to benignly neglect. They could change their mind without notice. Every girl like me put him into jeopardy. He would say so to supplicants who were in no position to hear it. He saved us despite our inability to see his humanity in it.

He looked at me and growled, "It'll cost a hundred dollars and I don't want her to pay it, I want you to pay it."

I said I would. I felt the hope in it, that my life might be salvaged. I would have promised anything. I would have promised even more hundreds of dollars I didn't have.

The abortion was done in his examining room on his half day. He couldn't use anesthetic because I had to walk out when it was over looking as normal as I could manage. His nurse was in the reception room. My mother was in his office. I lay on his examining table with my feet in the stirrups and my knees straddled. I did yell once and my mother came through his door, her face twisted with fear, straight into the sight of my spread legs and the bloody mess. Dr. Gore and I both yelled at the same time, telling her to get out.

At home, I cramped and moaned and my mother hovered in the small hallway outside my door, calling to ask whether I was all right. I didn't want her in the room where I hugged my pillow and lay in a tight knot. I was not all right and I was graceless enough to not keep it to myself.

My stepfather was remote, negligible, resentful. The couple would have quick flaring exchanges. She wished now she hadn't found the doctor. She was sure that something was very wrong, that I might die. My stepfather, a man with a usually gentle nature, was sure I wouldn't die and told her so, fiercely. No such luck, they'd have me forever.

One sunny afternoon I was being driven to Santa Fe by a friend. As we passed Dr. Gore's street he said, "I have to stop here for a minute", turned left and stopped in front of Dr. Gore's office.

"I won't be long," and he was gone.

I sat waiting, feeling anxious, and, as I had feared, the doctor walked my friend back out to the car. We were formally introduced. He recognized me but didn't let on.

We left, continued driving north.

One of the things I thought was that I hoped he didn't think this particular friend was responsible for my pregnancy.

On the drive to Santa Fe I learned that Dr. Gore was admirable, that he went regularly to the scattering of houses in Tesuque Canyon, alongside Route 66, and doctored the Mexican families there without charge. I don't know whether it was then that I learned he had been badly wounded during the Second World War and, like many who were given morphine for their pain, he had become addicted.

His addiction finally caused him to lose his license. He was arrested for misuse of drugs, found guilty, sentenced and put in prison. I knew about all this because Albuquerque was still a small town in those days. The local newspaper was bound to be moral about a doctor discovered to be a criminal.

When he came out of prison he got a job in a mental institution. He was hired as an "orderly" but used as a doctor. That might have given him some consolation, that he was needed. I hope it did.

He deserved better than that.

*

Absolutes

Absolutes are seductive; an outright tragedy, an outright comedy; one wants an end to all the ramification, the second thought hard on the heels of the first thought and then the second thought's second thought.

In all the daily push and shove it gets to where a pratfall is a laugh and a disaster is a rest with hope doing a half-baked tango back and forth between.

*

Adieu

I've just sold this house I've lived in for eighteen years. It sits on an acre of land along with three legal outbuildings and one illegal one.

The soil is so rich here that if a bird flies over and shits, there's a garden. Any seed that gets blown in here gets planted and grows. That's not uncommon in this part of coastline Marin. Flowers and bushes that in other places make gardeners despair grow wild here; they're called "escaped exotics."

The legal buildings are all a hundred years old. They are more dilapidated than they would have been if they had been owned the last eleven years by someone with regular work and an income. The buildings all need work for termites, powder beetles, dry rot, damp rot and the exhaustion of old wood. Lately when friends have come calling they have said things like, "I fell through a hole in your deck when I stepped on it. I put a board over it so no one else will step there."

The realtor described this place as being in a condition of "deferred maintenance."

When I came here eighteen years ago I had a husband, three children, a dog and three cats. Now I'm by myself, and the thought that anyone else might depend on me twists my insides in a knot.

That's not what I wanted to talk about.

I'm in the middle of all this accumulated junk, trying to be competent, planning yard sales and pricing U-Haul trailers, and I just caught myself on this early morning in January wishing I had the benign and blessed feeling of someone waving a chiffon handkerchief and crying out, "Adieu! Adieu!"

What I'm registering instead is bitterness, and anger at the energy it takes to keep from thinking about it. So much went so wrong it changed my cellular chemistry. When I think about it I sit and can't move, caught to grief and loss.

There are millions like me.

I wish it was in me to be nicer about it, more loving in the remembering. I wish I could go through a dictionary and take words out like buying a new wardrobe, assume a new style.

"Adieu! Adieu!"

I don't even know where I came up with that winsome creature. It never was me.

"Adieu! Adieu!"

The termite report doesn't mention mice, rats, earwigs, slugs, snails, raccoons, deer, quail, the red fox I saw sunning on the hill. It doesn't mention the Monarch butterflies that migrate through here annually; they fill the air like bits of flying stained glass and lie quivering on the ground in the sunshine, caught to forces, to sexual passion, to the need to move on.

*

Quotes: A

Four ducks on a pond,
A grass-bank beyond,
A blue sky of spring,
White clouds on the wing:
What a little thing
To remember for years—
To remember with tears!

—WILLIAM ALLINGHAM, 1828–1889

*

"All this buttoning and unbuttoning."
—ANONYMOUS
(Eighteenth century suicide note)

*

"The young are prone to desire and ready to carry any desire they may have formed into action. Of bodily desires it is the sexual to which they are the most disposed to give way, and in regard to the sexual desire they exercise no self-restraint. They are passionate, irascible, and apt to be carried away by their impulses. They have high aspirations, for they have never yet been humiliated by the experience of life, but are unacquainted with the limiting force of circumstances. If the young commit a fault, it is always on the side of excess and exaggeration."
—ARISTOTLE

*

The desires of the heart
Are as crooked as corkscrews.
The sky is darkening like a stain;
Something is going to fall like rain,
And it won't be flowers.
—W. H. AUDEN
(*The Witnesses,* 1932)

*

B

Beauty Contest: Ms. More Usual Person

A Beauty Contest I might have a hope of winning would include as values: chewed-up fingernails; hair with split-ends, matte finish, unlikely color, tired roots, and exhausted curl.

A pretty girl is like a melody...

(Well, sort of like a melody... A not so great melody... A melody that never quite resolves its beginnings into a negotiable middle and then on into a usable finale.)

That haunts you night and day...

(Haunts is a good one . . . a real pale face that doesn't invite a vigorous tan, as in a vampire that can't stand to be touched by sunlight . . . I mean, any light, any light at all can drastically interfere with the delicate patina of my personal charm.)

That haunts you night and day... Just like the strain of a haunting refrain . . . She'll start upon a marathon and run around your brain...

(Yeah, that's the gist. When I really get my grip in it's like that, like I really look good when I start upon a marathon and run around your brain . . . with my chewed-up fingernails and my pale but interesting face, and my really drab hair.)

She'll start upon a marathon and run around your brain.. . You can't escape... She's in your memory... Morning, night and noon ... (We're starting to get close to it now, to what I really require if I have a hope in hell, me and my hairballs and my frazzled-out wash-the-color-in-it's-good-for-six-weeks—that's six times you wash it and you're back to nondescript and it's time to start over again— me and my hair going through our six weeks up and down, running through your brain, you can't escape ... I can see where you might want to, I mean I'd like a little relief myself, six weeks in, six weeks out; you think beauty is easy?

Why isn't it like school, where the teacher graded you according to what you started with and how much you made out of it. Where the kids who were brilliant had to do even better and the ones who didn't have a hope in hell were given a little encouragement. Misleading, sure. Not the way to toughen up the young for the streets of the world. More like a brief breather, with the implication that Authority operated on the lost-sheep ethic where the lost lamb gets desperately looked for and there goes God getting enthused about here comes back that one lost sheep. And the teacher looks past the class geniuses writing genius papers and checks me out, dyslexic, can't read, can't write, live in a trailer with my mama and daddy here from the old countries can't even understand each other's language; the only thing I have to read is joke toilet paper we bought on sale because of the typos. My book, I call it.)

Just like the strain of a haunting refrain . . .

(Oh my god, the strain, the strain, of a haunting refrain . . . I'll start upon a marathon and run around your brain if that's what it takes.)

She will leave you and then, come back again . . .

(Tenacity. That's what us beauties know all about, tenacity. Beauty is not easy to come by and it is not simple to maintain. Starting at the ground like a beautiful little plant, let's go up and up: Toes, Ankles, Calves, Knees, Thighs, etc. You know, and I know, that there's more than that to beauty. It isn't enough to have the parts in place. Beauty is when the parts work in wondrous harmony with the current social desires running a hardline counterpoint. So let's get into stuff like *rhythm* and *cute* and Hedy Lamarr

and Greta Garbo, Marlene Dietrich . . . There she is, Ms.
Amerika . . .

Aw hell, I don't know. It's all so overwhelming.

You have to start small.

You have to start somewhere.

I've been working on my hair for four weeks this time.

I'm just ready to go from Rich Dark Brown to Heaven's
Own Purple, what the hell.

I'm ready to get down to business here.)
She'll leave you and then, come back again,
and come back again,
and come back again . . .

*

Burnt Park

For many years the most space-consuming building in the
town was an overpriced Italian-food-fish-grotto restaurant
named Lambardino's. It was owned by Mr. and Mrs.
Lambardino, who came from Sicily and spent their lives
putting every egg into this one basket that would return
them in their old age to Sicily, to live like millionaires.

The building bent and twisted itself into every available
bit of space. It was added on to, reconsidered, taken away
from, reconsidered further, and was, when it stopped, a
rambling warren of unmatched rooms; to consolidate the
whole mess and make all the pieces hang together it was
painted a rich pink.

All that transformation used up the Lambardino's time.
They grew old making plans. Their dream of Sicily and
retirement was still twenty years away. Mr. Lambardino
continued his daybreak-to-midnight schedule: buying sup-

plies, overseeing the kitchen, acting as resident entertainer, holding forth loudly on anything that caught his attention, waving his arms.

Mrs. Lambardino lived her daytime life in a wheelchair, dressed in a replica of the waitress's uniforms. She was a permanent sour-faced fixture in the dining rooms, her eyes small and mean. She watched the waitresses with a hateful expression on her face that showed she didn't believe even her watchfulness could keep them honest. She was filled with the acid knowledge of waitresses who didn't note down the garlic bread, who brought extra sauce from the kitchen, who knew what demands could be made by legitimate customers and passed them on to friends as "perks." And she watched to see that waitresses didn't pocket their tips.

I was getting gas at the station one morning when the woman who had waited on us the night before came over to say, "Thank you for the tip you left last night but you should know that we don't get to keep the tips."

"What happens to them?"

"We have to turn them in."

"Can't you drop them in your pocket?"

"If I got caught I'd be fired. I really need my job."

Most people liked Mr. Lambardino. Nobody liked Mrs. Lambardino. And Mrs. Lambardino liked nobody. She sat and glared. It was too late for Sicily. It was too late for anything but to be an old woman in a wheelchair, in a green waitress uniform with beige collar and cuffs in a pink restaurant where every room had a different floor level, surrounded by customers who would cheat if they could, by employees who would cheat if they could, with an old husband who . . . and looking at him her face would gain a further dimension, the accumulation of soured years, an old woman in the wrong country in the ruin of all of it, all of it.

She did finally die and Mr. Lambardino was left to plan for Sicily alone.

Every morning at six he was in the restaurant's small front room at the lunch counter to give coffee and breakfast to people on their way to work.

One morning at five past six I was there as well, for sustenance. I wanted coffee. Maybe I'd even have breakfast.

"What're you doing here this early?"

"I've been fighting all night with my husband. I decided to leave for awhile."

"You marry," he shrugged his shoulders, "you fight. Me and my wife, we had a fight every day for fifty-three years. So what else? Did you expect something else?"

He watched me, waiting to hear just what kind of a fool I might be.

"Yeah, I guess I wanted something else."

"Wanted! You wanted! Sure, we all wanted it different! Everybody wants it different. But nobody gets it different. That's *marriage*. That's what it is. Everybody gets it that way. You know anybody got what they *wanted?*"

"Yeah, I see people that look like they're happy together. I see people that don't fight all the time."

"They're *liars*. They keep it hid. They do it where nobody can see them do it. When they're with people they smile, but it isn't any different with them."

"Aw, come on. It isn't *always rotten*. There must be some people who should be married to each other, who're happy."

"*Nobody! Nobody* has it different. That doesn't mean they shouldn't get married. That doesn't have anything to do with it."

"You figure we weren't put in this world to be happy?"

"I don't know why we're in the world. You think not being married would make you happy?"

"I think not being married would have let me sleep last night. I wouldn't have had to fight just because somebody wanted to fight."

"There'd be something else. You don't have to marry trouble to have trouble. There's plenty kinds of trouble."

"I didn't come down here to argue with *you*. If I want to argue I can go home."

"You call this an argument? This is talking about something. If we were having an argument you'd know it. If I was arguing with you, you wouldn't be able to stand it. I've been a fighter from when I was born. I came out of my mother kicking and yelling and I haven't changed since!"

"Well, you're right. I'm not that good at it. Let's talk about something else."

Mr. Lambardino filled my cup and changed the subject by about half an inch.

"You knew my wife?"

"I never *met* her. I saw her in the restaurant."

"In a wheelchair?"

"Yeah, she was in a wheelchair."

"That was her. We came from the same village in Sicily. She had a temper. She would fly off the handle over *nothing*. Over *nothing!* And me, I had a temper. We both were hotheads. When we got engaged, people in our village started making bets on us. They said we wouldn't stay together a month. Plenty money on it. Everybody from miles came to see us married. They were all interested. Like watching the start of a horse race. They all smiled and wished us happiness and all that and looking at them you couldn't tell which way they had betted.

"Me and her, we got to our bedroom and the first thing we did, inside the door, before we took off any clothes or kissed or anything, was we made a pact that we would stay together for a month. We weren't going to let anybody make money on us. A month! We both agreed. We didn't want for anybody to make money off of us."

He gave me some more coffee.

He said, "By the time you've lived with somebody for a month you can live with them for the rest of your life.

"By the time she died she couldn't do anything for herself. I had to take her to the bathroom, I had to wipe her. I had to bathe her. And finally I had to take her to the hospital because I couldn't swallow for her. She couldn't swallow. And she couldn't go to the bathroom. They put all these tubes into her and out of her. All she could do was lie there and they did whatever they wanted to. She never stopped suffering from the time she got to the hospital. She begged me to take her away, to bring her home and let her die, and they wouldn't let me. They said it would kill her to take her away. It took her a long time to die."

"That's awful. That's an awful way to die."

"That's the new way to die. That's how everybody is going to die from now on."

"I hope it doesn't happen to me."

"It's going to be *worse* for you! It's going to be *worse* for you! They're going to *know more* by the time you die! They're going to be able to keep you alive longer."

Mr. Lambardino did make his try for Sicily.

He sold the restaurant.

The deal was in escrow and he was still in charge of the place when he burned it down.

Late one night, March 21st, spring equinox, two or three in the morning, he turned a full barrel of some kind of oil over onto the floor, let it run and spread; and set it on fire.

He didn't think at all about the people asleep in three small apartments on the second floor. Somebody woke up because of the smoke or the noise Mr. Lambardino was making, banging around, trying to put the fire out. He had changed his mind.

He was rescued, black from smoke and distraught. He was taken away in an ambulance to the hospital, to be treated for smoke inhalation and burns. Then he was taken to Napa, to be treated as a "mental" case.

He escaped from Napa, briefly; it was written up in the newspaper. The town cheered, thinking that even as they were reading the story, he might be on his way to Sicily.

That was a vain hope. There wasn't any money. His burning the restaurant down had invalidated the insurance.

And besides, there was the reality he must have faced in that late-night-darkened kitchen; all his planning had shrunk to going to a foreign place to die among strangers.

When the paper told us he had been found it mentioned that he was being put in a locked ward.

In the middle of the small town there is a hole where the pink restaurant was, a big bite bitten out of the town.

It's called Burnt Park.

*

Bumper Stickers

"Hi! I've been waiting for you. Look at this, we've got the *same* bumper stickers! Isn't that amazing. Three out of five. We've both got *Your Karma Just Ran over My Dogma* and *You Can't Kill People by Pointing a Finger Unless You've Got a Trigger under It.* Then we both dump on Reagan. You've got *What Did the President Forget and When Did He Forget It?* and I've got *Ronald Reagan, Too Dumb to Be Guilty.* Now is that unlikely or what? I thought, 'Georgina, you've got to meet this person male or female as the case may be.' What's your name?

"*George!* I can't believe this. *My* name's *Georgina!* Talk about *Fate* in the Lucky Super Market parking lot!

"I see you've got *Gentle Men Let Strong Women Do It to Them.* Does that mean your preferred sexual partner is the opposite one?

"Oh boy! Well, tell me, George, are you married? I don't want to be pushy, but would you like to come to dinner sometime? My God, what's going on? Look at all the cop cars!

"Right now? Well, I wasn't thinking of anything *quite* so *impetuous!*

"George, it really is not convenient for me to go with you right now. I have to get my groceries home and I have a consciousness-raising class at three.

"It is an *unwarranted assumption* on your part that I want you to come home with me *now.* But I *would* like you to come to dinner. Sometime. Are you a vegetarian?

"Oh, you are *not* a vegetarian. You *are* a bank robber. You're a bank robber?

"*You're a bank robber!*

"You've held up *two* banks and killed *eight* people . . . you *stole* this car!

"You want me for a hostage? Being a *hostage* is a very passive way to relate to . . .

"George! That's a gun! You've got a gun! Do you have *bullets* in that gun?

"Well, all right if you *insist,* but George . . . I think you should turn around.

. . . .? . . . .!!

"It's true, George. He *does* 'have the drop on you.'"

"What a relief. Thank you, officer.

"No, this man is not a friend of mine! We were simply discussing bumper stickers. Bumper stickers.

"Oh, George, does this mean you *like* Ronald Reagan?"

*

Quotes: B

"'Tis better to have loved and lost, than never to have lost at all."

—SAMUEL BUTLER

*

* C *

John Cage

I heard Cage once, talking to music students at a university. One student was outraged by Cage's approach to composing, taking it to imply that all the time he had put into learning the conventions was trivialized. Cage said, "You have to distinguish between the old music, which was a music of concept and of the presentation of that concept to us, and the new music, which is percept and the arousal of perception in us."

He was somewhat victimized by audiences who thought his theorizing meant permission to join the performance. In San Diego he stopped a concert to tell the audience they were spoiling the music.

He visited our house in Buffalo once and went next door to ask the woman there whether he could have the mushrooms he had noticed growing in her yard to put in the spaghetti sauce on the stove. The woman said he could have them.

Her children watched while he carefully pulled the mushrooms. They had asked him why he wanted them and he had said he meant to eat them. They watched with the breath-catch they would have given any man about to be the victim of an accident. They stood at the side of the potential event.

Cage has a story of a visit he made where, when the mother of the household served some of his mushrooms to her children, who had watched the preparation, they burst into tears.

*

Challenge

"Sharing" leaves me cold but the first time I heard "challenge" when I'd have said "problem" it went straight to my heart, a word that lets you be desolated but implies options, every destruction an opportunity.

I don't know what my character would have been if I hadn't had so many opportunities to improve it.

*

Quotes: C

"I am not at all the sort of person you and I took me for."
—JANE WELSH CARLYLE, 1801–1866
(letter to Thomas Carlyle)

*

"When I was little I believed that foreigners could not really talk at all, but were only pretending."
—JEAN COCTEAU

*

* D *

Dogs That Bark And Will Not Stop

Dogs that bark in neighborhoods, off through the walls, beyond where you can place them, marking the air into shapes with their beat of bark . . . bark . . . barkbarkbark . . . bark.

*

Quotes

"We will now discuss in a little more detail the struggle for existence."

—CHARLES DARWIN

*

DEATH AND DYING

O Death, where is thy sting-a-ling-a-ling,
O Grave, thy victoree?
The bells of Hell go ting-a-ling-a-ling
For you but not for me.

—song popular in british army,
1914–1918

*

E

Enroute

Maggie felt an instant disaffection at the sight of Henry's pale blue canvas shoes with crepe rubber soles and the faded blue denim pants that were not faded at all but a commercial color. Given all that, Henry's boyish and knowledgeable face was predictable. Still, there he was, no help for it. Chance encounter is one of the joys or at least one of the mind-broadening aspects of travel. Maggie sighed.

They watched him cross the brief time span of the brightly colored tile floor. One of their children was at each of his sides; Alice to his left, Karen to his right.

He had come to save them from their ignorance.

"Only *Indian* children play in the park," he told them. "You're a writer, aren't you?" he asked Patrick, recognizing his name as an afterthought.

"Is it dangerous?" Maggie asked Henry, meaning to understand where her children could play. "Can they get hurt."

"Well, no."

He meant good taste and status.

She told the girls they could go out again to play in the park. "And don't talk to strangers," she added, too late.

"I've read some things of yours," Henry told Patrick and was thus identified as a reader of obscure literary publications.

He was a tenured professor, he stressed "tenured" with a wry look to show he felt his shackles, of "Creative Writing."

"Good money in it?" Patrick asked, his eyes half-closed, whether because of the sunshine, Henry, or exhaustion was hard to tell.

"Oh, yes. Well, the going rate."

Henry was on Sabbatical, which meant that he was currently being paid to *not* teach Creative Writing.

Henry's house, to which he invited them, saying their children could play with his children, was a hollow square of rooms all opening onto a central courtyard. It was filled with children and a woman with gray hair, introduced by Henry as "my wife's mother, Charlotte."
The two oldest children, a boy and a girl, were distinguished from the others as the children borne to Henry by his *first* wife.
"I married the first time for love," Henry said bitterly. "I never made *that* mistake again."
He took them through a medieval kitchen, rotting and damp, into the kitchen yard to meet his second wife, the mother of his five most recent children. She was washing clothes in a tub.
"This is where the servants stay," Henry said, and laughed to show it was a joke. Mrs. Henry didn't laugh, didn't stop washing clothes, didn't look up when Maggie tried to chat. Maggie was no more than an interruption in her career of being Henry's unloved wife.

It was finally being too long a day. They were too tired to requalify the original proposal, which had been that they go with Henry to his house "for what we laughingly call 'comida.'"
"Comida" was a long time coming.
In the buzz got from sharing three seventy-five-cent bottles of wine, did Maggie worry that her fine Patrick had a recognizable gleam in his eye, was in the beginnings of one of his notorious bits of drunken behavior and would, in all likelihood, direct it toward ghastly Henry?

She did not.

Every move Henry made defined him as deserving another treatment than his defaulted household gave him.

Henry's ménage also included a pimpled plump young man introduced by Henry as Charles, his "star pupil," who would "be a really good writer, someday." The implication was that it was Henry's tutelage that would mold Chuck's pathetic clay into a finer form.

Henry reintroduced his original theme, the issue of the children playing in the park; the prestige of persons like himself, in the outback nations. It suited him, born to be free and own it.

When Henry sent Chuck for more wine, Maggie went along.

"If these marks aren't on the label," Henry said, holding an empty bottle for Chuck to look at, "don't let him sell it to you. He'll try to tell you it's the same but it's not."

At the wine merchant's the shopkeeper looked puzzled while Chuck, prepared to kill for quality and his master's voice, earnestly examined the labels. The marks were there. Chuck treated it as a personal coup.

"This is all much too much trouble," Maggie said to Henry and to Mrs. Henry. She longed to return to the nice little hotel. "I'm sure it would be more convenient if we came for comida another time."

"I know she's slow," Henry chided Maggie's impatience, "but she does only have one servant to help her."

Mrs. Henry glared at Maggie, then turned back to her husband for instructions. She stood near his shoulder, her eyes on him as intently as if he were the cliff she hung from.

"This is something I assigned my freshman class last year." Henry passed Patrick a sheet titled *Principles of Enjambment.*

"You use enjambment?" he asked as Patrick blindly scanned the page.

"I do enjamb, Hank," Patrick said seriously.

"Why does your husband call him Hank?" Chuck asked Maggie. "Henry *hates* to be called Hank."

"That's probably the point, Chuck," Maggie answered.

"What?"

"I said, 'You said it, Chuck.'"

"What?"

Comida was beans and tortillas, wilted lettuce, potatoes, coffee. It was not laughable.

"Okay, Hank," Patrick rose with the finality of a brown bear rearing onto its hind legs, "it's time for the cantina."

Before they left, Henry added a thirty-one-page poem— "romantic theme, ballad form, personal innovative method" —to the stack of items given over for Patrick's consideration. Patricks being caught here until Tuesday meant there would be time to discuss all of what was close to Henry's heart. Patrick turned the pages in quietly increasing despair.

"Lots of enjambment in there, Hank," he said.

Henry smiled, then frowned.

The cantina was one room, three wooden tables, a dozen rough chairs, a jukebox, a light bulb hanging at the end of a cord; every table had a lighted candle in the depths of a tall glass with a religious image decaled on the outside.

Maggie stopped at the hotel to see the children to bed, told the young Indian girl that she would be at the cantina, three doors away.

The three men were at the table lighted by the Virgin of Guadalupe. The candle had burned far enough to be a glow in her belly.

Chuck was nervous. He licked his lips and looked around the almost-empty room, telling his story to Maggie in a babble. He had had bad experiences in Mexican bars. He wished the lights were brighter.

"They'd just see you sooner, Chuck," Maggie reassured him.

Patrick was also looking around, gleeful, looking for the action. If there was any action to be had, Patrick would find it.

The way of a man with a maid is an endless source of wonder. Henry, who had specified his wife as the woman he need never love, still had notions of romance. He began to wall his eyes in Maggie's direction. He caused a lugubrious rendering of "Cuando Me Ti Quieres" to play on the jukebox.

"I like Rancheros," Maggie said.

Chuck's fears were proven justified.

He came crashing against Maggie, skittering his chair sideways. The space he had cleared so adroitly was filled by a drunk who had crossed the floor, intent on their little group.

The man's body, even when he had stopped, kept a slow roll of motion as if the floor were in heavy seas. He leaned forward against the table, floundered, and looked, his lip snarled and ugly, at Chuck who looked back.

"Gringos!" The "s" spewed over their heads as the Mexican continued his glare around the table.

Chuck was crawling into Maggie's lap, his head turned to look back.

"He means trouble," Chuck was whispering as he crawled. "He's going to cause trouble."

The Mexican continued his sneering way around the table until he saw Patrick.

There is a vast understanding among drunks. Like dogs and small children they recognize one another across all barriers and their faces tighten to attention. All else fades into the background.

Patrick waved one arm in a splendid gesture.

"Y pues!" he announced to his newest long-lost friend.

"Y pues?" the standing drunk was understandably confused.

"Y pues!" the seated drunk insisted.

The Mexican reached to the next table and dragged a chair across the bit of floor to put it in the space so recently vacated by Chuck, who sat shivering and terrified by his new neighbor.

They made a charming picture, Patrick and the Mexican. The Mexican's arm was laid over Patrick's shoulder and left there while the Mexican talked, his face screwed into a villainous expression, his mouth spitting. Their faces were a scant inch apart. At intervals the Mexican would wave his free arm at the other three and glare and Patrick would also look at them, his face angelic and delighted. A friend at last. Whenever the Mexican stopped talking as if he had asked a question, Patrick would say "y pues" and bob his head sympathetically, and after a moment of puzzlement the drunk would continue.

Maggie's ears were being hissed into, Chuck on one side, Henry on the other, an ear apiece. They were telling the same story: catastrophe in stereo.

"... he just picked up the beer bottle ..."

"... hadn't done *anything* ..."

"... straight for the face ..."

"... three men to hold him ..."

The Mexican stood. His chair fell over behind him, crashing against the floor. Chuck and Henry flinched as if it had been a gunshot. They were ready to go under the table. The standing Mexican glared at them with venomous intent that stopped short of murder but who could guess why. He leaned toward them, putting his hands on the table. They were transfixed. Their faces registered horror Hollywood would have paid for.

"Gringos!" he accused them, spewing them with spit.

He took a long time straightening up, his eyes still on them.

Upright, he glanced at Maggie. She wasn't in his argument. He looked at Patrick. His face melted into a tender regard. He lifted his right hand at the end of its arm in a soft flourish of farewell, a gesture as pure as an entire ballet. He turned and left, a shambling creature.

Chuck pulled his chair back into place.

"Why did he like *you* so much?" he asked Patrick, jealously. It was a burden to him that the Mexican nation went for his throat on sight.

"Well," Maggie stood, "I'm for bed."

She felt no pity for Henry's obvious anxiety at whether he was being left responsible for Patrick. Life in the fast lane, Henry.

She said goodnight to the duo, gave Patrick a kiss, and left.

The weather still held.

Maggie walked through the warm air to the hotel, gave the girl who had watched the children some money, changed the baby's diaper, went to bed.

"He *threw* me out of his house!" the wail of Patrick, misunderstood. "He told me, 'Leave!' He said, 'Go home, Patrick Dougherty!'"

The room was dark with a seepage of light around the door. Patrick was on the floor in a semisprawl, as he had fallen.

"*I* said," the dark lump moved as if toward a more dignified position, "*I* said, 'You understand this means that the next time we meet I must *kill* you!' And *he* said," Patrick gave up any attempt at dignity, laid flat and chortled, "*he* said, 'then I must do my best to avoid seeing you!'"

They decided not to wait for the highway to be repaired. It was all too possible that while that landslide was being repaired others were happening elsewhere. They decided to drive back down the mountain, cross to the Pacific coast, put the van onto a flatcar and be carried across the border on a train. There would be no landslides to contend with. It would be more trouble but they could depend on it.

They began to gather their belongings.

Patrick decently laid the manuscript to one side before he ripped all the other things Henry had given him to pieces.

"I looked at Hank's wife and her mother waiting to be told they could go to bed and all I could think of to say was 'Hank, enjambment is shit.'"

They finished loading the van and sat in the patio for a last cup of coffee. The older girls were having a last run in the park.

Chuck, perspiring and worried, came through the door on his latest fetch-and-carry errand.

Patrick went to reclaim Henry's manuscript from the owner of the hotel.

"I've never *seen* Henry so upset!" Chuck told Maggie.

"Would you like some coffee?" Maggie asked.

"Oh, no!" Chuck backed away.

Chuck would be asked for an accounting when he returned. Hank wouldn't take kindly to any fudging.

Patrick returned, handed over Hank's epic; Chuck was free to go, and did, in a hurry, relieved and sweating.

Maggie said, "I wish I had a couple of borrachos with busted beer bottles to see that boy home."

Patrick was out in the van, hoisting the bags around, when Chuck came back.

"Henry wants the examples of enjambment," he announced, his voice firm and righteous, the voice of Hank coming through by remote control.

"Patrick tore them up," Maggie said, smiling and friendly.

"He *tore* them *up?!*"

"He tore them up."

"It was the only copy Henry had with him!" Chuck's face was built for bad news. "He's *really* going to be mad!"

When the van was packed, the girls were called from the park. The family climbed into their places. The motor was started. They began the long descent toward sea level, through layers of warmer and warmer and hotter air.

*

Quotes: E

Ecology

> In Köln, a town of monks and bones,
> And pavements fanged with murderous stones,
> And rags, and hags, and hideous wenches,
> I counted two-and-seventy stenches,
> All well defined and separate stinks.
>
> Ye nymphs that reign o'er sewers and sinks,
> The river Rhine, it is well known
> Doth wash your city of Cologne;
> But tell me, nymphs, what power divine
> Shall henceforth wash the river Rhine?
>
> —SAMUEL TAYLOR COLERIDGE

*

F

Fatalism

Fatalism allows disappointment to think it's thinking; to
have a philosophy.

*

Frog Story

Pat Skye told me that a friend of his, an animal behaviorist,
got a shipment of frogs from Africa at his lab and was
unpacking them from cardboard boxes. In Africa they
have a kind of frog that can grow to weigh thirty pounds.
A mutual friend was with him watching him unpack the
frogs and said, "Do you know that day after tomorrow is
the annual frog-jumping contest in Calaveras County?"
   The two men looked at each other and the animal
behaviorist said, "Riiiiight."
   Two days later, with the biggest frog from the shipment
in a cardboard box, the two men set out for Calaveras
County.
   The frogs that go to Calaveras County to jump are
aristocrats. They have histories of bloodline on their
mother's side, their father's side. They live and travel in
glass-enclosed environments. Their diets are taken seriously. The traveling case that surrounds all this is necessarily
large. The frogs are, comparatively, small.
   The animal behaviorist and his friend were carrying a
very small box, but inside it was only frog.
   They got teased for the size of their box.
   "You kidding? You really got a frog in there? Let's have
a look."

They showed their frog to no one, the old Ace-in-the-Hole, and continued to be a not all that interesting joke: the guys with the little box. They registered and laid low. Frogs are jumped one-on-one in that contest. It stays intimate and personal. The form, to be more specific, is that owners have elegant little prodding sticks. Three prods, totaled, is a jump.

Their turn came. They stepped forward and their opponent saw he had got the weird guys. Perhaps he felt a flicker of alarm, after all, the unknown . . . More likely he didn't, took it in his stride, put down his frog. A frog with generations of jumpers behind it.

Now it was their turn to put their frog down. They opened the cardboard box, rousted out the thirty-pound frog and put it down on its little circle. It covered the circle.

The gathering went aghast. Somebody went for the official rule book. There was no rule disqualifying thirty-pound frogs.

Meanwhile, bedazzled by light and heat, jet-lagged, all the way from Africa with hardly a pause to pee, the very big frog sat in a lump and had a look around, a horizon of feet and ankles, so this is what it has all come to, and finally saw something familiar—its opponent. With a quick flick of the tongue and a slurp it swallowed the little fellow down.

And was disqualified.

*

Quotes: F

THE FROG

What a wonderful bird the frog are-
When he stand he sit almost;
When he hop, he fly almost.
He ain't got no sense hardly;
He ain't got no tail hardly either.
When he sit, he sit on what he ain't got almost.

—ANONYMOUS

*

"What, after all, is a halo? It's only one more thing to keep clean."

—CHRISTOPHER FRY

G

Golden Gate Bridge

Oct 19, 1987, the day of the Monday Massacre/ Meltdown Monday when the stock market dropped 500 points; and at this end of the nation deputies were assigned to the Golden Gate Bridge, to watch out for jumpers.

*

Gossip

Apropos gossip being made a dirty word by people who are not addicted to it, I say to hell with that.

One of the really good things about gossip is it doesn't imply more than that somebody thinks they know something. And everybody takes it with a grain of salt, because it's gossip. Try taking *psychology* with a grain of salt; it would be like telling the examiner during the Spanish Inquisition that you think the Bible is interesting as literature.

I'm not going to dwell at length on the righteous non-gossipers who purse their mouths like a chicken's asshole when they're demonstrating the standards of saying nothing.

My friend, Joe Bacon, is a Southerner from near New Orleans. When he gets set to gossip his face positively glows.

In Houston, Texas, he drove me past the house of the woman who got the biggest divorce settlement ever recorded and who said, when she was interviewed about it, "I did it for women everywhere!"

And Joe says, "And she said that, honey, without cracking a smile!"

*

* H *

Heart

You know the kind of tourist who speaks the language badly but does it fast and loud? Anyone who doesn't know the language thinks the spill and flurry is the language being spoken properly. Until the look on the puzzled faces of the natives makes it clear they're only confused, can't understand what is being said to them: we're being conned by a tourist.

The heart has language and place; the heart has tourists who pass by pretending to mean something.

*

Householders and Health

Picture a couple sitting on a couch, holding hands, late at night. They are in their home.

It is late fall. The dark has come early. The lights are lighted and in the kitchen the dishwasher is washing their dinner dishes.

Their television is on. They are watching a program on ecology.

The couch they are sitting on is foam rubber, possibly carcinogenic, possibly a factor in sterility in males. The couch cover is a mix of cotton and something that lets it be washed easily. It has been sprayed with chemicals that keep it from absorbing stains. Their feet rest on a carpet of petroleum derivative. The drapes are also a petroleum derivative. Petroleum derivatives are notorious for inducing allergies.

His chest is slightly congested. He is trying to stop smoking. She has hay fever and is looking forward to the winter when all that lively stuff that plays hell with her nose is dead, dead, dead.

On television the commentator is listing food additives that should be guarded against. The program is sponsored by a health-food store that also sells health appliances. A commercial comes on for stationary rowers and stationary bicycles. Muscles that are allowed to deteriorate can make the body feel that it is rotting, an old piece of fruit left in a bowl, beginning to grow thalo-green mold, undesirable however beautiful. Bodies that are unused haven't even the advantage of wonderfully colored molds. Bodies that are unused become lumpy and misshapen, unattractive. People who feel unattractive limit their sexual activity, feel awkward and exposed and repulsive. Feeling repulsive has the effect of a spreading stain, it extends to one's normal daytime world, makes one shy and nervous, can cause the fingers to twitch and oneself to feel like a caricature from a Dickens novel, can make one self-involved in a counter-productive way. One's job can suffer. Nervous twitchers don't get promotions.

The dishwasher runs the wash water out and begins to rinse. The powdered soap that is most effective in dishwashers is filled with harsh cleansers. It could never be used in a normal dishpan with human hands doing the work. That is the advantage of the machine. The hands need not be made raw and sore by being in contact with the soap. If the dishwasher is good enough to rinse the dishes thoroughly, it will also be the case that the stomach will not be harmed.

As a public service the television is listing ways to make the kitchen safer. The kitchen is the room in the house where accidents most often happen. In the kitchen the (sharp) knives gleam in their holder near the stove. The (explosive) gas stove waits for a light. Hot (scalding) water is poised in the tap. There are electric (!) plugs nearby for all the small appliances.

Because it is a cool night the windows are closed, the gas central heating is on.

Indoor pollution proliferated when householders responded to the fuel shortage and the rise in heating costs by insulating, by weather-stripping doors and windows, making their homes airtight. Now the indoor pollution is often higher in well-to-do houses than it once was inside factories producing asbestos.

The couple we are watching is a two-salary family. They have an eclectic assortment of furniture: Danish Modern, Sears Baroque and Almost Antique. It is variously stuffed, covered, and finished. All the odors of new cloth and varnish are being held in their well-insulated living room and breathed in and out, over and over, as the couple sit. The health-food store advertises an air purifier.

The couple owns their environment. They own the floors under their feet, the walls with doors and windows that hold the ceiling and roof over their heads. Their house has small patches here and there of termites, powder beetles, and dry rot. When they can afford it the entire house will be covered by a plastic bag and be so intensively poisoned that all the pests will be killed. Some of their more ecology-minded friends have warned them that the gas does leave a residue, they can expect to be living in a poisoned atmosphere for awhile.

The dishwasher turns itself off with a soft whine.

None of these perils loom paramount in the couple's mind. When the health-food store advertises herbs and vitamins to combat the destructiveness of stress they don't pay much attention.

They are happy.

They are happy to have found each other, to be in their new house with their new furniture. They are young and modern. They met in a singles bar and were delighted to learn that they both are market researchers. It's great to have something in common.

They yawn as the television set announces its next disaster. They smile at each other, stand, take turns in the bathroom (the second most dangerous room in the house) and go upstairs.

They will go to bed among allergenic bedding and make love, with all the sexual partners either one has ever had hovering like dark angels, and they will go to sleep.

It is hoped they will dream. Research shows that people who don't dream are headed for trouble.

*

Quotes: H

Happiness

"Mourning the loss of someone we love is happiness compared with having to live with someone we hate."
–JEAN DE LA BRUYÈRE

*

Heaven

Here lies a poor woman who always was tired,
For she lived in a place where help wasn't hired.
Her last words on earth were, Dear friends I am going
Where washing ain't done nor sweeping nor sewing.
And everything there is exact to my wishes,
For there they don't eat and there's no washing of
     dishes...
Don't mourn for me now, don't mourn for me never,
For I'm going to do nothing for ever and ever.

> —Supposed to be an epitaph found in
> Bushley churchyard before 1860,
> destroyed by 1916. Quoted in a letter
> to The Spectator, September 12, 1922.
> I doubt it. Can you believe it?
> Carved in stone?

*

* I *

Interviews

My favorite story lately is: In Boulder, Colorado, Allen
Ginsberg was interviewed; he was asked whether there
were any hot young writers around that he would care to
name.

He said, "Oh, there are always a few young Rimbauds
around."

Which got quoted as " . . . a few young Rambos . . . "

*

J

Mrs. Florence Foster Jenkins

Mrs. Florence Foster Jenkins, "the noted if controversial coloratura soprano," gave the most celebrated concert of her career on October 25, 1944, at Carnegie Hall. The performance was sold out, including standing room. Scalpers were peddling tickets at twenty dollars. More than 2,000 people were turned away and police were in attendance to keep out gate-crashers. All to hear a concert by a seventy-six-year-old woman who could not carry a tune and had no sense of rhythm.

She was one of the great jokes of the time. Some of her performances were simply an audience laughing from beginning to end. She was undaunted, never thought of herself in any but the most serious fashion, believed the laughers were a claque paid to disrupt her concerts by other singers who were jealous of her success.

One lot of reviewers loved to carry on the joke, writing things like, "Mrs. Florence Foster Jenkins gave her usual riveting performance," " . . . in better voice than ever," "Her attitude was at all times that of a singer who performed her task to the best of her ability."

Other reviewers were more truthful: "Her singing was hopelessly lacking in semblance of pitch," and "She was undaunted by . . . the composer's intent."

She was notorious for high notes that continued to rise beyond her ability to make them heard. The "listeners" would watch while Mrs. Jenkins continued to sing without any sound whatsoever. After a while the music would return to lower registers and she would return from the void.

She was dubbed "the first lady of the sliding scale."

Her career began when she was forty-one years old and her father, who had refused to let her go to Europe when she was seventeen and study music professionally, died. She had never let that early dream die. With the money she inherited she began to stage her own concerts, hiring halls and paying all the costs, with the proceeds usually going to charities, often to needy young artists.

She had many admirers, among them Enrico Caruso, who felt that her spirit was unique.

When she was asked how she felt about her bad reviews she said, "Some may say I couldn't sing, but no one can say I didn't sing."

She died a month after her concert at Carnegie Hall.

*

Journal . . . Mazatlan

August 15, 1968 . . . Mazatlan
The Playa Hotel was where we thought to stay, described by the travel agent as the only hotel right on the beach, as particularly as if he knew; when, in fact, there were at least a dozen hotels right on the beach.

All of them filled with tourists wearing assorted tourist drag.

It became personal to us that they were all so filled when we checked in. Our travel agent had mismanaged our reservations. We could stay for certain only for this one night. We were told to ask tomorrow at noon whether they had an opening.

Some agent.

So there we are. Caught in the clutches of terminal dumb.

But for now, sweating and jet-lagged, we only need think of pleasure.

We joined the vacationers who were shifting like loose seaweed in currents, being managed by the management. The management provided drink, they drank; music, they surged to it; chairs and tables, they sat.

And were subjected to the sophistication of the management's waiters who had seen them a million times before. The waiters were filled with contempt for these gringos who tried to speak Spanish, who waved their hands hoping to draw the words they would never know out of the foreign air.

The only thing the waiters respected about the gringos was their money. The waiters showed their respect for the money by keeping it.

Painfully sunburned faces puzzled through this latest mystery. "Was that the price?" they asked each other, husband and wife, dressed in fabrics that pictured flowers and palm trees, holding drinks filled with pieces of fruit.

"Is beer five pesos?" someone at the next table called after an oblivious young man who passed quickly, busy, busy.

The couples were dressed in their play clothes. Good children don't fuss.

"He must think it was a tip."

Husband and wife both relaxed. They could also think of it as a tip.

Travel is broadening. They are travelers, big-time spenders however inadvertent. They smile at the waiter, having been generous. They've come to have a good time and they're having it. The young waiter, seeing they had relaxed, smiled; very white teeth. They smiled back. It's a relationship. Despite his press of work, his rushing about with full and empty trays, he had singled them out for his flashing smile. Their generosity had paid off. They believed the little mistake would ensure their having better service.

They had postponed, though not for long, their bitter revelation. In one more day their manner would have changed to a sullen acceptance. Their broadening experience would see to it that their pockets and purses held a clutter of change. They would count and recount the strange coins, looking closely at numbers while the waiter waited. And when they ran short and had to give the man a note they would join the others calling "Cambio!" loudly after the hurrying figure who, short of physical threat, would never hear them.

What else caught our jaundiced eye, knowing we needn't like the place.

The "decor"—pebble mosaics in a "modern" pattern on the lobby walls, a fountain alongside the staircase with the cement basin painted turquoise blue, an aquarium wall to separate the bar from the lobby. All of it common and usual, the look of a fast-food chain restaurant on any freeway.

We were too disillusioned to find the vulgarity charming in itself.

Some agent.

There were other features: our shower leaked, the plastic wastebasket had been put under it to catch the rusty water. Did that imply a plugged drain?

(In fact, the day we arrived was not August 15th. We arrived earlier, on the 12th or 13th, it seems to me. August 15th was the day I began this journal. By August 15th we had gone house-hunting, had been taken over dirt roads by a sympathetic taxi driver in a junker of a car, had gone a far distance along the beach, out of the fashionable tourist area to a hotel just opened.

It was simpler, no waiters in cummerbunds, no orchestra.

It was more our kettle of fish.

We returned to the original hotel that second day at noon to say that we had found other accommodation.

Ah! But there was a room for us. A better room. A room that overlooked the playa.

No, thank you, we said, we are well pleased elsewhere. And left.

We had escaped the travel agent's assorted ignorances.

If anything went wrong henceforth it would only be a mistake of our own making, more acceptable.

So now, we have arrived at . . .)

August 15, 1968
Were there ever other birds, more ungainly, less able to skitter over the wet sand, food gathering, who died for it, leaving only these thin-lined birds, sandpipers, as querulous as they are graceful, finicky, jerking their heads about in irritation and disgust when they are unexpectedly caught by a wave and must walk through foaming water, dull as pedestrians, step by step, back onto the shining sand.

(That new simpler hotel had as its only luxury four thatch-roofed cabañas to give shade. They were a decent distance apart, and there were few enough guests to let us be territorial, stake out our choice, have chairs and a table brought out into the bit of shade, hang a new-bought hammock.)

A family, the mother Indian-looking in a soft white dress, the father, both young with sweet faces. She has a frizz of permanent in her hair, making it a dark halo around her round face.

The father is at the water's edge, the mother and the three younger children are stationed higher up on drier sand. The oldest child, a fragile and feminine girl, runs from one parent to the other and back again.

The mother is on a chair, holding the baby. At her feet are planted three bottles, one of red soda, one of orange soda, one of beer.

The second-oldest child is a boy, foursquare, running in considered circles, significances and fierceness in every move, pushing sticks into the sand, stabbing the sand. His younger sister toddles nearby, sits abruptly, stays there sifting sand through her fingers.

On his mother's lap the baby's head is tilted far back so he can watch his mother's face while she talks to him or turns her own head to watch her husband and daughter on the far wet edge of sand where it meets the water, to watch her son be fierce, to watch her daughter letting sand fall through her fingers.

They are here to watch the sun go down.

The sky, earlier, when it looked as if it might rain. was marbleized; shapings and clusters, whites, grays, yellowed brown, all had outlines glowing a brighter white at the edges from the sun they hid.

They have gone, the mother, father, and son who arrived three days ago.

"He's an invalid of some sort," Bob had said of the son, and it certainly must have been so. The boy, who was perhaps fifteen, had arms and legs as thin as sticks, his torso was a stick; his shoulders were those awkward blocks of bone jutting far out from the neck to be seen in concentration camp pictures. But it was his manner that was the most strange. His gestures were articulated as if he were a puppet. He looked dressed as a puppet looks dressed, his shirt and pants very pressed, his hair glued down. He had new sandals that he wore even in the invasive sand. He carried a camera and took endless photographs of the barren new hotel.

It was that that had stopped them here, the father told me—I can't remember how the conversation originated—that the building was "new" and "clean."

Only the father swam. The mother, plump and self-involved, went into the water only as deep as her knees. She was not, apparently, afraid, but was so stopped and secured it was clear she meant to go no deeper. She stood there looking toward the horizon, watching the waves come toward her so as to back into shallower water when it seemed they might come higher up her legs. She wore a pale blue bathing suit.

The father, in the range of her gaze, waited for the big waves, the slashing ones; he would throw himself onto them and ride as far as they would carry him.

The boy also went into the water, fearfully, removing his sandals, to stand ankle-deep. It was a terrible challenge for his courage. At first he had frozen in place as each small wave, its strength dissipated farther out, lapped at his ankles. Then he had begun to move, to wade.

We had first seen them three days earlier at eight in the morning, when we came out. They had invaded the cabaña we thought of as ours, with our chairs and table, our hammock, my book on the table.

"What can we do about that?"

"They don't know they can get chairs from the hotel." I went to tell them and realized that something was very wrong.

"They're all nervous. They won't look you in the eye. They looked all around me and up and down but they wouldn't look at me."

And Bob, looking at the thin boy, had said, "He's some kind of invalid."

We went back into the hotel to give the newcomers a chance to resettle themselves without our threatening presence. When we came out again they had taken the cabaña to our right. They had chairs and *two* tables, one holding bottles of Coca-Cola, the other, cameras, binoculars, oddments.

That first day had been the most difficult for them. The boy had been the most stiff, walking back and forth between the cabaña and the hotel and the cabaña and the water's edge in his stiff little puppet steps. The man and woman spoke not a word to each other. She spent most of the day in the hotel.

And the boy went wading, for the first time, in the shallows, taking incredible angled stances against the small waves that reached him.

We watched, not even wanting to see, his private battle. He would come into our line of vision, wading, a small ripple of wave would approach and, *en garde*, he was prepared! Let them beat at his ankles, they would not take him down!

The second day had been better.

On the second day the boy had not gone farther into the water but he had gone onto his knees; it had *seemed* that he was in deeper water. He had let the water come up onto his thighs. Then a slightly larger wave had made a stronger backrush, sucking back toward the ocean and he had leaped up in alarm, arms and legs akimbo, ankle-deep.

A vendor passed and the father bought a hammock to sling in the shade of their cabaña, and a woven green palm leaf hat with a bright paper flower attached for his wife who by now had returned to their room. He gave the hat to his son who carried it across the hot sand to the hotel, presumably to give it to his mother, trying it gingerly on his own head as he went.

Later in the day there was some kind of a scene. The boy sat in a chair, his head in his hands, while the father squatted alongside, talking to him and talking to him. The boy sat unmoving, his head in his hands. The mother lay motionless in the new hammock, took no part in the conversation, gazed upward toward the thatching. Her new hat, rampant and colorful, lay on one of the small tables, next to her large, white, shining plastic purse which later, the boy consoled, she asked be handed to her; as the boy lifted it he began to examine it and very carefully ran his hand along each of the smooth sides in turn before handing it over.

August 16, 1968
The man from New York and his wife, whom Bob instantly loathed because they "knew" him when he had meant to know no one. I had asked the wife the time, not wanting to walk back to the hotel, so it was my fault that we were all caught into a tedious exchange of New York fact. I think she wanted it as little as I did, but it was as if, somewhere, a bell had rung, as if a pair of vaudeville hoofers coming on stage, pretending to stroll, had gone into rehearsed steps on a given signal, intricate but predict-

able rhythms, with their mouths fixed in smiles. Anyway, introductions passed around as politeness.

And now Bob hates the man, sights him in the water far away, can recognize him at incredible distances, the only man who "knows" him, and whom he "knows" in return.

(In the morning we would wake, shower and dress, go to the sparely furnished dining room for coffee and whatever else we wanted, return to our room, change into bathing suits, drape towels over our shoulders, burden ourselves with an assortment of books, pens, notebooks, cigarettes, sunglasses, suntan lotion, whatever, and stroll out of our room directly onto the sand. It was one of the pleasures of the place that we were on the ground floor and faced the ocean.)

(In the evening before the sun had started its proper move to sunset we would walk along the beach, north and west, the ocean on our left, until we came to a restaurant that was only a floor and uprights holding a roof. The walls were token walls, rising to table height. We would have our evening meal there. The sunset, according to our timing, occurred while we were walking one way or the other, or while we were eating, the colored glow of it lighted us evening after evening.)

"Don't go in the water!" the man from New York called out to us as we walked past. "Our youngest boy got badly stung by a jellyfish. They're washed up all over the beach!"

But we saw none, and the usual number of people were swimming.

"Wouldn't you know in all of Mexico *his* kid would get it!" Bob said.

Coming back along the beach we saw the New Yorkers swimming. The mother and father were coaxing the son who had been stung back into the water.

They hadn't gone, the family of three. They had taken down their hammock for the night, and now are back again, the son in the reinstated hammock, the mother in one of the chairs with her feet up in another, the father, who at this very moment has turned on a transistor radio—a new addition—an insistent Mexican trumpet, as if someone screamed but then, no, it's a melody.

It seems as though the wind is blowing in even, timed gusts but really it's whether the hammock is swinging with it or against it.

The pelicans skim flat and low over the water but I haven't seen one go into that free-fall downward that ends with the bird somersaulting in the water and, at the end of it, bobbing on the water's surface and stretching its neck out long to swallow its catch.

The hotel owner's son, a thin young man, is growing a thin young moustache and practicing dignity.

Shifting their positions between the hammock, the chairs and each other, the family of three is taking photographs; the father of the mother and son, mother in the hammock, son behind, his arms making stiff triangles to his hands on hips, painful and studied. Then there is one of the mother in the hammock with the son in front trying a casual hand on one of the cabaña's vertical supporting poles, which then becomes two hands on the pole, not so casual, which becomes, as the father raises the camera, the son holding desperately onto the pole trying to cover over his desperation by pretending to examine it, studying the pole with care and great interest as if it is a discovery. When the picture has been taken the father touches the boy's shoulder to give him the strength to turn loose.

And later, in the late afternoon, the boy went deeper into the water, went into water just above his knees. In the new threat, the danger he had chosen, he returned to his John L. Sullivan approximation, his fists raised, his legs crouched against the water.

But it was an act of courage, a farther move, chosen by himself.

Is he winning in all these small confrontations?

Can he win?

Are we seeing a convalescent return to health? Is all this a return to happiness in a story we can only vaguely guess at?

August 17, 1968
One of the five sandpipers who make a group in their beach scouting has a bad leg, the right one. It gives him a soft dip to that side in the quick skating short-stepped run they all use.

He's not slowed by it and there seems to be no handicap in terms of pecking order.

The five are a unit. One of them seems to be, if not a leader, the active warrior, and yesterday got rid of another intruding sandpiper by chasing it down the beach. When it lifted and flew but not far enough the protector also lifted and flew, landing near the other bird with a thump of landing, as if it had gained weight in the flight. The intruder stood still and the attacker began an aggressive walk towards him, giving sharp pitched, squawking cries. The other bird flew again and it was all repeated until the other bird had gone beyond eyesight, when the fifth sandpiper of the pack flew back and resumed his scurrying feeding.

(What is being left out of all this is the two of us. We are invisible to me now, looking back.

If one is complicated by nature there is a reward in finding someone equally complicated. Usually, there are all those floating tag ends, what doesn't get used up. Exhaustion is more likely than boredom, an exchange that seems worthwhile.)

(But in this blessed instance of which I speak we were not exhausted. We were in heavenly truce. We drifted in vacation, walked along the beach hand in hand or with an arm around the other's waist.)

(History does not hold. I once believed in it, but even the most sacrosanct dates memorized by generations of children are not trustworthy. Historians constantly alter the story, having come by further information. They stay right. They never *are* wrong, they only *were* wrong. The past, for historians and their consummate overview, is malleable, holds no threat.

But one's own history . . .)

August 17, 1968
The beach where we spend most of the day is between our hotel and the ocean.

The name of our hotel is The Cantamar, The Sea Song? or The Singing Sea?

We sit daily in a thatched-roof beach house about ten feet across, shaped in a circle formed by driving eight posts about four inches thick into the sand at intervals of three to four feet. They stand about seven feet tall and at the upper end of each is a natural crotch. Eight slightly smaller poles lie across these crotches to make an octagon. From these joins, eight thinner, longer poles rise at an angle to a central peak. Smaller poles are laid across these and form the base to which palmetto leaf is attached, tied on with lightweight rough twine.

We look directly out onto a flat horizon of the Pacific and sometimes see ships crossing there as particularly silhouetted as if they are cardboard cutouts. The ocean lifts so the horizon is at eye level. The ships have only passed from right to left. They cross our view very like the objects that cross to be shot at in shooting galleries.

Closer than the horizon, less than a mile, to the left and to the right, two islands of similar size and shape rise up out of the water. They are one shade of green where the green is grass, and a darker green where bushes grow and, perhaps, low trees.

The island to the right is slightly larger, lumpier, more of a piece; the island to the left has a higher center but more slopes and, on its right side, toward us, has a long grass meadow.

After this length of time, looking at them, I feel sensitive to their look as if it were their name.

Children can conceive of luxury, as the child who takes a chair down to the water and sits there in the wash and pulling away of every wave.

Waves, at midtide, are slower in frequency, do not collide, so each wave rides a crest of white foam far up onto the sand. If you are near enough, as that child is, you can see that the bubbles of foam hold rainbows.

When the waves are very strong they scoop darkening sand in the downward circle of their motion. If you are body-surfing and your timing falls short you can find yourself caught into the pull and push, thrown against the ocean floor.

Reading this second-hand copy of *Mrs. Dalloway,* I find I am irritated by the marginal notes written down by some student—"orgasm," "human nature," "unifying spirit."

I got the book in New York City when I had an hour to kill before Bettina's Brecht concert, then didn't need it. So it has taken me this long to realize how costly that sixty cents I saved was/is.

Yesterday, at lunch time, where we eat, a fifteen-minute walk along the beach, three young Mexican boys came up to look over the low wall at us, sitting at our table. They were natural clowns, for us and each other. They had a perfected act meant to charm us, but only because it already charmed them. They loved their own style, doing it. They didn't need us at all; we were the excuse.

The boy who looked to be the oldest, eleven perhaps, and the boy who looked to be the youngest were brothers. They were both gifted with mimicry à la Cantinflas, grandiose gestures dwindling into little flares of ludicrous failure. They egged each other on.

The third boy looked pure indio, round-faced and serious, very brown, intent, looking like a small-scale fully grown man, the perfect buddy, an appreciative audience to their fooleries.

We offered them Pepsis. The youngest boy came instantly climbing over the wall to accept. Knowing the proprietor to be a man of dignity, we suggested to the other two that they come in through the door.

The trio were an instant crowd.

The smallest, the live wire, neglected his Pepsi to dance a kind of improvised tango on the deserted cement dance floor. The prime issue of his style seemed to be whether his trousers, great baggy things, would or would not slip to the floor when he sucked his stomach in.

The older brother aped a grandiose notion of himself and his drink. He required a glass and ice and a straw; given them, he went through a pantomime of exaggerated contentment, sighing, sipping, examining his glass.

The Indian boy drank his Pepsi with no show, watching the brothers solemnly.

And we realized we might have made a mistake, might have saddled ourselves with more than we intended. We had finally to stop watching them. The most minimal response spurred them on. They were on the town. It became a question whether we could go on about our lives without them.

But they solved it, or their energy did. They drank the Pepsis, fell into a few final antics and left.

And now so could we.

We left thinking ourselves clear only to find we were caught in a pincer; the boys were in front and the couple from New York materialized behind us.

We must try to not walk faster than the three boys and not walk so slow that we were overtaken.

We failed. We caught up with the boys, but our fears were groundless. They didn't mean to stick with us. They had a whole population to bestow themselves on. They left us at the Mar-Rosa, a trailer court where many young Americans, men and women, stay in cars and campers and tents for a dollar-fifty a week.

Half a dozen hammocks swing, filled with one or two bodies. The owner of the trailer court sells marijuana at

Mexican prices. The tenants are, therefore, uncomplaining, languid, content. The perfume of the place fills our noses as we walk.

The enviably idyllic frame of mind evidenced by the persons we see, passing, is ripe for the trio of boys, the traveling road show.

The boys stopped off, we outdistanced the New York couple, who were doubtless as relieved by it as we were.

At the Cantamar we relaxed into our chairs to begin the long afternoon.

Later in the afternoon two horses passed. The riders looked to be father and son. Behind the father, a devilish pleasure on his face, rode the younger brother.

"Where did you want to get off?" the father was yelling back to him in English.

The older brother was chasing after the horses.

Still later they returned, walking jaunty, owning it. As they passed the cabaña used by the New Yorkers they stopped long enough to make use of the binoculars on the table. They looked out at the ocean, up and down the beach, masters of all they surveyed. They returned the binoculars to the table, being gracious and charming throughout. And returned to their sauntering along . . . how does it go? *with an independent air / I can hear the boys declare / he must be a millionaire.*

Shortly afterward the buddy came following, carrying three large green coconuts.

What else? Bugs collecting in the square of light outside the door.

(The last night we were there we walked out into the dark, to look at the moon and the water.

I was wearing a white cotton dress, a dress made in Mexico, with bands of lace set into the fabric.

The bright light behind us, from the hotel, cast our shadows toward the water. We walked on our shadows. They grew longer with every step. The dress I wore showed the bands of lace, where the light shone through, as if a shadow could be decorated.)

*

K

Franz Kline

Franz Kline's mother never trusted his choosing to be a painter. She wanted him to sell antique furniture as a sideline. She thought the money he made as a painter could set him up in a shop of his own. When he was at the peak of his fame she would write him letters saying, "It's still not too late."

When his father died and she was in the oppressive adjustments of widowhood he wanted to give her a pleasure cruise. Her response was, "Franz, you know I have never enjoyed pleasure."

*

Quotes: K

"Leopards break into the temple and drink the sacrificial chalices dry; this occurs repeatedly, again and again: finally it can be reckoned upon beforehand and becomes part of the ceremony."

—FRANZ KAFKA

*

L

This One's For Linda Joy

It was on Good Friday just after five in the afternoon when the phone rang.

I was living in my barn then, in the ragtag of leavings from my whole life that had come crashing down around me. Everything was musty and damp and cold. Northern California. I started every morning by making a wood fire in the stove.

But the latest rainy season had passed. Spring was here. The days were getting longer. Things were in the yearly turnaround that blesses humankind.

And the telephone rang.

"Hello?"

"Hello, Molly?"

"Yes."

"This is Linda Joy!"

"Linda Joy who?"

"Your *cousin* Linda Joy! How many Linda Joys do you know?"

It was true I didn't know that many.

"Where are you?"

"I'm here. I'm in San Francisco. That is, *we're* here. I'm traveling with a *male* companion."

She said it in the teasing tone that left it to me to make something of it if I was going to. She knew I wasn't going to ring any Texas Baptist bells in on her. Not with my history and inclinations.

"That's the best kind," I said, and then, "Are you staying in a hotel?"

"We just came for a weekend so we started out in a hotel, but by the time we'd been here that long we knew we wanted to stay so I've rented an apartment."

"You have an apartment in San Francisco?"

"I do."

Linda Joy was forty-four years old. She'd lived her whole life on the flat Texas plains within an hour of Lubbock. So far as I knew this was the first time she'd ever got as far as California.

It stood to reason that she was traveling with somebody. The story of Linda Joy's life was that somebody else owned it. First there had been her mother. Linda Joy's mother adored God and knew for a fact that God adored her back. She had God's ear even on things as trivial as whether Linda Joy was minding her manners. It must have been intimidating to know that any difference of opinion with her mother was going straight to heaven on the nightly prayer hotline.

When Linda Joy was sixteen she swapped her mother for her husband.

She was sucked into it that both of those people loved her and wanted the best for her. They both doted on her, at length and remorselessly.

Her payoff for sitting still and being the object of their affection was that she got to be "spoiled." Her daddy had a few square miles in irrigated cotton and her husband had a few square miles in irrigated cotton plus a few herds of Black Angus cattle, so being spoiled meant Linda Joy had just about anything she wanted if it could be bought.

It looked like her life would be spent in an uncomplicated and provided-for fashion, but she started having what got called *nervous breakdowns*. Cars and clothes and appliances and a new brick house with air conditioning were apparently not answering all her needs. Every so often she'd try to kill herself and be hospitalized, then she'd come out looking fragile and her mother would fuss over her and her husband would fuss over her and her psychiatrist would double her appointments. One of the gauges for her being "cured" was that she would regain her natural optimism. The people taking all that care of her would relax back, and there she'd be, in the same place.

People who have "everything" usually ask for more.

"Every time I saw you when we were growing up, you were walking around with a book in one hand and an apple in the other, looking for a place to sit," she accused me once. And she said, "Jack and I have joined a reading club. Every month we all read a good book and then we all get together and talk about it. I told Mama, 'Now I know what Molly was up to all those years.'"

"That sounds worthwhile," I said.

"You always had the advantages," she said wistfully.

"I don't see where you figure that," I said.

I don't want to go into my childhood at any length, but in a nutshell my father was brutal and a woman-chaser, and there was never enough money. Shoes and doctors and winter coats were a large problem. We moved from one town to another every four or five months. Whenever we went into a new place my mother would wipe down the mattress, getting into all the crevices with turpentine or kerosene. Whole nations of bedbugs snugged in and waiting for their next meal were dispatched by my mama's righteous hand. When my father was home there would be more money, paid for by fear and violent scenes, things crashing and broken, a lot of noise.

Linda Joy, on the other hand, went shopping with her mother every late summer for the coming year's school clothes: five new dresses so she wouldn't be shamed by having to wear the same dress twice in the same week, plus skirts and sweaters, school shoes and dress shoes, school coat and dress coat. And when she was in high school she had her own car.

I envied her. It looked like heaven to me to live all my life in the same house with my own bedroom and ruffles around the bedspread.

All I really had to call my own was that book and that apple. The apples were probably healthy but too many books can poison you. Too many books gave me an elevated notion of self-importance. I decided I was some kind of an artist. That *decision* is often the only choice people who are "artistic" get to make. However much they pretend it's an option, their selves are often all they've got in the bank.

"I know you never had much money but you had the *worthwhile* things. You had *books* and *Art*," Linda Joy said, and smiled.

In addition to her book club she was learning how to paint in some women's group. She was convinced that we'd agree on the value of Art.

"Damn, I hate Texas," I snapped back at her. And of course it hurt her feelings. How could anybody hate Texas?

I wasn't talking about Texas at all. I was reacting to the squirm I felt around my kinfolks when I was invited to appreciate their latest sortie into *Art*. I loved my people but I hated that squirmy feeling.

When I hit puberty me and my folks went at such tangents that they never again took me as normal. Whenever I'd visit they'd haul out their Art as a kindness, like talking to an Eskimo about ice.

The last time I visited my cousin Lonny he showed me a rooster in profile, made by gluing different kinds of beans onto a masonite board. He pointed it out to me that it made a difference whether the beans were glued down flat or whether they were turned on their edges.

I just went along, a compliant hypocrite, discussing bean technique like I was protecting him from some horrible further knowledge, resenting it all the while that at my approach those damned products of the paint-by-number kits came out.

I couldn't help noticing that the rooster looked a little mangy. There was a soft fuzz around some of the edges. Some kind of mealybug had seen those beans for what they were and the rooster was being eaten away.

"So when I made one for Mama at Christmas time I varnished it. Nothing's got into that one."

We stood there, them feeling happy and sure of themselves and me being the one that was out of place, telling Lonny and his wife and his mother that it was wonderful, that rooster, and what a shame the worms had got into it, and what a good thing he'd known enough to varnish the next one that I hadn't seen yet but would see at my aunt Eubie's house.

However many books Linda Joy read, however many canvases she covered with copies of landscapes she would never see and Indians she had never seen, her nervous breakdowns kept pace. And she kept on thinking that having just about anything she wanted when she was sane enough to ask for it meant she was leading a good life. She took her breakdowns to be occasional interruptions in the best of all possible worlds, like having the hiccups.

Her psychiatrist told her when she was in her mid-twenties that she "suffered" from "pre-menopausal depression."

"If you had been in your teens he would probably have said your depressions were pre-pre-menopausal," I said.

I hated it that she took everything he said as gospel truth, but she never had been encouraged to question bosses.

"Billie Sue *likes* Jack," she told me, a twitch of disgust at the corners of her nose.

"Well, I should hope so, " I said.

"No, I mean she *likes* him, like she's a woman and he's a man."

"Is that more of that psychiatrist you're going to?"

Billie Sue was about ten years old. I hated to think of the damage that fool of a "professional" was doing.

While Linda Joy's history kept repeating itself, her life, as lives will do, went right on ahead, with or without her.

Her kids grew up.

Her husband fell in love with his secretary.

There was a divorce.

Linda Joy moved into a condominium in Lubbock.

And now here she was, having just made the first long-distance call she had ever made in her life without putting it through the operator. Of course she gave Blue, her "male companion," the credit. He had told her how to dial me direct and she had done it.

"Well, where *is* your apartment?"

"It's right downtown. I'm right downtown." She named a street that I've forgotten now and added, "I'm on the eighth floor."

"When do you think we're going to get to see something of each other?" I asked her, and she started telling me about her bank.

Her bank was supposed to stay open late on Fridays, and that afternoon she had taken a little nap.

"... and I had plenty of time, according to when they *said* they'd stay open until, but when I got there they were closed."

"So you're calling me because it's Good Friday and the bank's closed and you're out of money and you can't cash a check until next Monday?"

"I got there in *plenty* of time, according to what they said their hours were."

"I guess I owe it to the bank that I got to hear from you."

"I was going to call you this week."

"Okay, I'll tell you what. I'll drive in tomorrow morning and pick y'all up and bring you out here for the day ... that is, if you'd like to come?"

"We'd like that."

"Do you have money to eat on tonight?"

"Oh lord, yes. I'm not completely helpless."

"Then I'll come in and pick y'all up in the morning. You can spend the night here if you want to and go back into the city on the bus Sunday. We can get a check cashed for you at the grocery store." I added, "It's going to be good to see you, honey," and I meant it.

"Me too. I'm looking forward to it."

I hung up the phone and no time at all went by before I thought that if Linda Joy was living here she was going to find out that I was a writer.

And if she found out, everybody in Texas would get to know about it. Everybody meaning all the relatives I'd managed to keep it secret from.

The first book I ever wrote was about my relatives in Texas. I wrote down some of the stories I had heard all my life, from when I was little and the stories were being told after supper by the light from a coal oil lamp in the middle of the cleared-away table, through later on when I was big and the light had been electric. The technology changed but the stories stayed the same. When I went to write them down they went onto the paper word for word, like automatic writing.

Then I started to worry about whether I had got it right, whether I had turned their talk into some kind of half-baked dialect. I didn't want them to sound like Hollywood hillbillies because they weren't.

So when I took a trip back to Texas with my mother I took along a small tape recorder in my purse. My reasoning was that whenever I meant to write on the book I could listen to the tape first, listen to their real voices and get the right tone and tempo into my head.

Once the tape recorder was there, there were all the new stories as well, a bonus, like my cousin Lonny talking about how worshiping the devil could give you the ability to turn newspaper into dollar bills.

All along, my notion of those stories was that later on I could improve on them. It was a lesson in humility to learn that they were better left alone.

I finished that book and somebody decently undertook publishing it. As the publication date drew near I started stewing about what I had wrought. I started waking up out of nightmares at three in the morning.

I'd lie in that damned damp bed in that damned cold barn and stare into the dark and think about how much my relatives were going to hate finding themselves in this book and how much they were going to hate reading what the others had said about them. In the course of driving around and visiting, it had naturally happened that people talked about whoever wasn't there. And there I had been, a natural fool with a tape recorder.

I could go on at length about why I felt guilty, but instead I'll just tell you some of my late-night justifications. Everybody in the family had already heard those stories dozens of times—that's where I had got them. Nobody was being made public to their friends and neighbors because I had changed their names and I had changed the names of the nearby towns and even the counties. I had left the state be Texas, but I couldn't think of that as a giveaway.

It still wasn't enough. I decided that I just had to keep the book a secret from my kinfolks unless I wanted my relations with them to get even more complicated.

Then I decided I had to tell my mother. I owed it to her for her years of believing I'd accomplish something some day. I called her on the phone and said that in about a week I had a book coming out and it was about all of us.

She said, "Oh Molly, everybody's going to be so pleased."

I said, "Well, that's what I wanted to talk to you about. I think it'll be better if they don't know about it."

"Why not, honey?"

"I tell about stuff like when Uncle Odie was in the Vet's hospital and Evelyn took his money and spent it."

And my mother said, "Oh."

The book did come out, time passed, it looked like I had got away with it. And here, with one telephone conversation as its messenger, came Discovery.

The next morning I got into my beat-up old vw and drove in to the city.

Glorious sunshine was making a showpiece of one of the world's truly beautiful ocean coastlines. The bright sails that proliferate in good weather filled the bay as I crossed the Golden Gate Bridge.

Once when friends of mine were halfway across that bridge they saw two men in evening dress seated on either side of a folding table that was covered with a white cloth, candles, a wine bottle in a silver cooler, wine glasses, having an elegant time of it, toasting the San Francisco skyline.

The address Linda Joy had given me was right downtown. Every car parked in the vicinity was about fifty feet long. I didn't have any trouble parking right in front of the building. I just fitted into what they all thought was throwaway.

The building came fully equipped: a striped awning out to the curb, a doorman dressed like a foreign general, an elderly woman in a short mink cape looking like all she ever did was sit in the lobby waiting for the limo to be brought around.

A soundless elevator with wall-to-wall carpet carried me up so smoothly that when the doors opened at the eighth floor I thought I hadn't started yet.

I had called before I left to ask Linda Joy to be ready because I didn't know whether I might have to double-park. She opened the door and we gave each other a big hug. She introduced me to Blue, very blond and good-looking. He was almost twenty-two. They'd met when he sold her a pair of shoes. I'll bet it was in a high-flash store. Whatever else he might be, Blue was not tacky.

We took one quick turn around the apartment and were set to leave.

To come out to stay with me for one night Linda Joy and Blue were carrying a packed medium-size Samsonite suitcase, a garment bag with half a dozen hangers showing, an overnight bag, and a large cosmetics case.

On the way down in the elevator I told Linda Joy, "Honey, you're in for a culture shock."

I've never felt at home in California. It is too beautiful; the senses grow calloused in self-protection.

One evening I was sitting on a wooden bench at sunset watching the colors change and the pelicans fly in long lines from the right to the left, toward the lagoon. Below me the waves foamed in soft rhythms on the sand, and I thought, "That's why Californians get so laid-back, they're perpetually besieged by the landscape."

But on that trip across the bridge, through Sausalito, over Mount Tamalpais, I felt like a proud parent whose child was being both beautiful and well behaved.

I have, after all, lived here more of my adult life than I've lived anywhere else. Perhaps there will be a time when the air comes to my nose with the sweet smell of home.

We arrived at my barn, the poor half-derelict building I sometimes think of as my Irish solution.

It had two rooms: the main room was large, maybe thirty feet by forty feet, with beams across at high-ceiling level and a pitched roof above: wooden shingles showed between the rafters, of course it leaked; and the second room, long and narrow, where the milking stalls had been, running the length of the back wall and extending farther. There was also a shed room I had turned into a sauna with a tin wood stove, and a bathroom with a toilet raised over a fifty-gallon drum which was regularly emptied by the local septic tank man.

I've never been overjoyed by the distance between me and The American Way of Life. I don't take delight in being hardy as if it proves other values. It's just that when I cut the coat to fit the cloth it didn't include a flush toilet.

When we had brought all the luggage into the main room Linda Joy smiled at me and said, "Well, Molly, do you mind if I have a look around your house?"

I had forgotten that.

Among my kinfolks, whenever you visit somebody the first time the convention is that you get shown around. You stand in the kitchen while you're told, "This is the kitchen." You stand in the bathroom doorway and get told it's the bathroom. And on and on.

And you're expected to be complimentary and interested as you go.

"What a nice idea to make every bedroom a different color."

"I just love it that your boys' rooms are so rugged and your girls' rooms are so feminine."

"Where did you find all those little animals made out of glass?"

Linda Joy was undertaking to do her part in carrying on that tradition. It was an act of courage; there wasn't a glass animal in miles.

I didn't intend to walk her through my three rooms, so I just said, "Honey, help yourself."

She wasn't gone long.

Now it was up to her to say something complimentary. You have to know that I would never have put her on such a hook.

She said, "Mama always did admire your lack of love for material possessions."

"I don't know how in the world we're going to make do unless Jack gives me more money," Linda Joy said. "Jack took three of the farms and I took three of the farms. And I get half of the co-op cotton-gin money. But I never had any idea that San Francisco would cost so much."

"Linda Joy, you don't *have* to hire a limo to go out to dinner. You can call a taxi and the driver'll buzz your apartment when he gets there, and when you're finishing your dinner you can have the waiter call another one to take you home."

She took a cigarette out of the pack, tapped it on the table, put it in her mouth and sucked in. By the time she was sucking, a gold lighter was in Blue's hand and he had a flame at the tip. It was all casual, effortless, gracefully choreographed.

Who did I think I was anyway, offering advice to a duo capable of that kind of style?

"It just makes me feel so secure, knowing he's out there waiting," she drawled.

Linda Joy was smoking the longest cigarettes I'd ever seen. What she stubbed out and left as butts were longer than most people start with. Their length made them a natural menace. They would rest at an angle in the ash tray accumulating ash and getting top-heavy. When enough of the tip had burned away the cigarette would demonstrate some commonplace theorem of physics by tilting out of the dish and onto the table.

"And they're going to sue me over my lease in Lubbock. I just told Jack to take care of it. *Somebody* has to get all my furniture out of my apartment there and send it to me here. And I told Jack I have to have my car."

"How does Jack's new wife feel about him dealing with your problems?"

"She doesn't have anything to complain about. She's already got my house!"

"He's going to send you your car?"

"He said it should be here by next Thursday. It's a powder blue Cadillac. I got it when I went to Lubbock to live. I turned that maroon Oldsmobile in on it. After I get my car we can drive out here whenever we want to. I just *love* this little town," and she gave me a big smile.

She took another cigarette out of the pack.

"We made out our wills so that if I die Jack gets my three farms, and if he dies I get his three farms. Now if I had *all* the farms we'd be just fine for money."

"Don't hold your breath waiting, honey. Ex-husbands don't die. They thrive."

That night the three of us went downtown to have a few beers and listen to some music.

Linda Joy's style, her wig and full-face makeup complete with artificial eyelashes, her "casual" garb from Neiman-Marcus, Blue's natural elegance and ready cigarette lighter made them instantly interesting. They drawled their way through conversations telling everybody everything. They were charming.

People I'd never had any particular reason to talk to would come over to me with their faces glowing, "I've just been talking to your *cousins!*"

"Well, you wouldn't think at *his* age that he has a *plastic* anus," Linda Joy bobbed her head in Blue's direction. The person she was talking to agreed that it hadn't occurred to them. "That boy has had a very hard life," Linda Joy said sadly. It seemed to be the case. He had the same history of nervous breakdowns that Linda Joy had—half as many, but then he was half as old.

"We go to bed at night with half a cup of pills and we wake up in the morning with half a cup of pills."

Also, Blue's sexual inclinations had been a problem to him while he lived his life ass-deep in cotton fields.

"Oh yes," Linda Joy said, "it isn't just the *girls* I have to worry about with Blue; with Blue I have to worry about the *boys* too!"

Whatever their age and sex differences, they were more like each other than they were like anybody else in the room.

Linda Joy would come over to tell me about somebody she had just been talking to. "That's one weird old boy," she'd say and shake her head.

It never occurred to her that she and Blue qualified as rare. She did notice that she might be a little overdressed.

"I can see that I'm going to have to have a whole new wardrobe that's just for when I'm in California."

I still had the problem of the book I'd written on my mind and it was proving true.

I'd introduce Linda Joy to somebody, "This is my cousin, Linda Joy."

Their eyes would light up. They'd say "Oh! Really?"

She was bound to notice.

I had a letter from my mother, "Linda Joy has told Myrtle you wrote that book and she really wants to read it. If she gets a copy then Alma will want to borrow it and she'll get her feelings hurt when she reads that part about Evelyn taking Odie's money and spending it. So if you give Linda Joy a copy to send to Myrtle, take that part out."

I come from a family of Irish-Cherokee-Fundamentalist-Baptists. They believe in miracles.

Linda Joy's Cadillac was drastically electric. If you had the bad luck to be in the damned thing with the doors and windows closed when the battery went flat, you could die there.

Linda Joy and Blue liked to park downtown, walk away from the car and have somebody tell them they had left their lights on. The car had a timer that let it turn its own lights off. That car resisted visiting my town. It wouldn't turn off the lights the way it was supposed to. They'd come back and find a dead battery. By that time the garage would be closed. They wouldn't be able to open the trunk because it only opened electrically. They'd spend the night at my place in borrowed pajamas.

By the time they decided to get married, they had made a lot of friends. We were in the bar and they told somebody and the word got around quickly. Everybody, however much they liked Blue, figured it was him marrying Linda Joy for her money. He strolled around the bar with a glass of wine in his hand, chatting and smiling; Linda Joy sat at a small table, enjoying the attention; and one by one the various friends they had made tried to dissuade them. Blue would just say, "Linda Joy wants it and I want to make her happy."

Linda Joy asked me if I would go with them to the Civic Center north of San Rafael and be their witness. "I'd like to have somebody there that I'm related to," she said.

"Linda Joy, I'd be proud to be there, if you're sure that's what you want."

It was a busy day at the Civic Center. The nearest parking places were all filled. I was early, to be in time. I stood next to my car so they'd be sure to see me. Blue stopped the Cadillac long enough to let Linda Joy out and went on, looking for a parking place.

"Are you sure you want to do this, honey?"

Linda Joy was sitting sideways on the front seat in my car, her legs were poking out through the door, high heels pressing into the warm tar top.

She leaned forward, looking at me, "I'll tell you one thing, Molly—I never want to be alone again."

Theme songs from the past, catch phrases: *Who was that masked man* who stayed for his fixed hour of allotted time, climbed on his horse, rode away, a fading "Hi-Yo, Silver ..."

Hi-Yo?

I've never in my life met a man who meant to stay.

I watched Blue come walking toward us, dropping the car keys into the pocket of his jacket.

It's all too bitter, the taste in our mouths, what passes for solutions.

The county clerk was a real turd. He didn't know what was going on but he didn't like it.

Well, I didn't know that I approved either, but I knew I took sides if he was on one of them. I was the relative, the solid citizen, member of the wedding, and I snubbed him as firmly as I was able.

After the ceremony the three of us went to a restaurant in San Rafael for a wedding lunch.

Linda Joy rented a house for them and her furniture on the hill over Sausalito.

"I've always wanted to live in the mountains. And I just *love* that little village!"

She paid the whole year's rent in advance.

"Linda Joy, with that much money you could have made a *down payment* on the place. Then if you decided later you wanted to leave it, you'd probably make money on it."

"Molly," she said, "you just make my head hurt."

I make my own head hurt, as often as not. All I was doing anyway was what I had always done, acting like *practical* mattered, and Linda Joy was doing what she had always done, what she wanted to.

There was another phone call, late at night, in November. The rains had started up again. I was sick and coughing. My car was on the blink.

And the telephone rang.

"Molly, could you come over here and stay with me?"

"What's the matter, Linda Joy?"

"I've thrown all of Blue's clothes on the floor and when he gets home I'm afraid he's going to kill me."

"Where is he?"

"I don't know. He stole my car two days ago and drove off with one of his friends. *I've* got the keys. I guess he went into the dash panel and hot-wired it. I didn't know he knew that much about cars. And these Cadillacs are supposed to be thief-proof."

"Doesn't he have his own keys?"

"No. There *is* an extra set but I've got them, too."

"He probably had some made."

"How could he do that?"

"Didn't he ever take the car out on his own?"

"Oh yes, he did that."

"Then he stopped somewhere and had some keys made."

"I don't think he'd think of doing something like that."

"So he's on his way home now?"

"I don't know. He hasn't telephoned or anything."

"You mean you want me to stay with you for as long as it takes for Blue to decide to come home?"

"He's really going to be mad."

"I don't want to do that."

"I was *afraid* that was what you'd say."

"It'll cost about fifteen dollars for a taxi to bring you here. You leave a note and say you're here and for him to telephone when he comes home."

"I want to wait here for him because I want to get my car back.

"When I hear him drive in I mean to get ready, and when he goes into his room I'm going to run downstairs and get in the car and drive it off."

"You think that's a good idea?"

"Well, I'm just torn between my car and my furniture. I know that if I drive off he'll tear up my furniture.

"I've called Jack and he's going to come and get me and my car and drive me back to Lubbock. But he can't get here for two days. Blue's afraid of Jack."

"Linda Joy, how worried *are* you about him being violent? Do you *really* think your life's in danger?"

"I just know that he's going to hate it that his clothes are on the floor."

"It sounds to me like the first thing you'd better do is pick up Blue's clothes and hang them back in the closet."

"That *would* give me something to do."

"Then, tomorrow, call a mover and tell him to come get your stuff. That way when Blue does get back all you'll have to think about is yourself and your car."

"Well, that makes more sense than just waiting for him to come home and have a fit about his clothes."

"Now, Linda Joy, I want you to think about how safe you are there. If you're not safe you get a taxi and come here."

"If I hang his clothes back up he won't have anything to be mad about."

My aunt Myrtle called me when she learned about Jack's plans to come get Linda Joy and drive her back to Texas. She was worried that during the night they would have to spend on the road Jack would try to "take advantage" of Linda Joy. I proved my immorality once again by saying that if Linda Joy was afraid for her life what mattered was getting her somewhere safe. I think she had hoped that I might go along for the ride to act as chaperon.

The next day Linda Joy and Jack dropped in for a quick visit. We didn't talk about Blue or about Jack's new wife. They left the next morning. I'm sure that the night they were on the road wasn't spent in separate beds.

I get depressed at the approach of Christmas. Me and all the world, it seems. On the television and in the newspaper there are all the stories about desperate people. The mental wards fill up. The world is at its darkest.

In my barn, in the dark, the rats were back. That meant I'd have to go to the hardware store and get poison. Putting down poison meant, because the stuff is effective, that the smell of rats rotting under the floorboards would be around for awhile.

I had been writing in my bed and crumpling the papers that were to be thrown away so I wouldn't waste time by checking them out again. A pile of crumpled paper lay on the floor next to my bed. I was wakened by the rustling. Something in the papers. I turned the lamp on and looked into the face of a piebald rat, its eyes flamed red with reflected light. We froze, looking at each other.

This was the first time I'd ever seen one of the things. I hadn't known rats were that big and I had assumed they'd be a brown like mice. This thing looked more like a vicious mutant guinea pig. I made a move, and with a fast scuttle it was gone.

I was awake. I had things to worry about, now I could worry.

I worried about money.

Then I worried about all the things I'd done wrong with my life.

I worried about love, my lack of it.

And health, my lungs and sinuses, cancer.

My car, rusting in the rain.

It was about 3:30 A.M. I had plenty of time to worry about everything.

And in the dark cold room, the telephone rang.

I'll never know why Blue called me at that time of night to tell me Linda Joy was dead.

It might have been that I was the only one who would treat him like he'd lost a wife. I had been the only family at the wedding.

None of that explains the time of night he called. Anyone who sleeps badly knows the paranoia that settles onto whatever wakes you up. It often feels like malicious intent.

He meant to wake me up and he meant to give me the bad news.

Linda Joy had tried to kill herself with sleeping pills, again. They had never worked before. Maybe that was what had been proven, that she could suicide herself over and over again with sleeping pills and always live to tell the tale.

But this time in the hospital she got pneumonia. And she died.

I thanked Blue for letting me know.

I told him I hoped he was all right.

I got out of bed and added a wool sweater to my night clothes, put a bathrobe on top of it all. I took off my house shoes and put on wool socks, then put the house shoes on again.

I started a fire with the crumpled paper the rat had been walking around in, some kindling, some slightly larger pieces of wood.

I put the kettle on.

I was up.

In the morning I telephoned my mother. Then I telephoned my aunt Myrtle.

"Hello?"

"Aunt Myrtle?"

"Yes."

"This is Molly."

"Nora's Molly?"

"Yes, it's Nora's Molly."

"Where are you?"

"I'm in San Francisco."

"Oh, are you? Did you hear about Linda Joy?"

"I heard about Linda Joy. I'm calling to tell you how sorry I am."

"Well honey, Linda Joy's better off. She's at rest now. Her life was so tore up."

"Would you rather not talk about it?"

"I can tell you. She took some pills, you know. And they took her to the hospital. She was unconscious. And she come through and seemed to be doing good. We thought she was going to be all right. Then she took pneumonia and her lungs just give way, so she passed away. But she called for prayer before she died and they had prayer with her and the chaplain said he felt like Linda Joy made her peace with God. So that gave me a great comfort."

"That's good."

"Yes, it really is. How are you? How have you been?"

"Well, I've been sick. And I always tend to get depressed at Christmas time."

"You know when Henry passed away . . . he was buried eleven years ago today . . . he was buried on Christmas Eve day. Christmas sure don't mean anything to me. Nobody's doing anything about Christmas this year. But Linda Joy did have such a nice funeral and everybody's been so sweet to me."

"Mama thought Linda Joy and Jack were getting back together."

"Naw, they weren't. He separated from that woman, but then he went back with her. I think that's what caused Linda Joy to do what she did. She was tore up over him. If she had lived, I think she'd just have tried to kill herself again."

"Well, I just hope this is not too hard on you."

"It's not. I'm relieved that Linda Joy's at peace. But I miss her. I have some of her paintings, and that's something of her for me to keep. That's as much as I need of her. Blue's mama was at the funeral. And he sent some flowers. Poor little thing, he's all mixed up."

If I didn't laugh I'd cry gets said in every language everywhere.

Most of the stories I write are as funny as I can make them. Part way through, this story stops being funny.

For a long time I'd tell people the first part of this story. It was like I could overlook what came later, like Linda Joy was still alive. But sometimes, whoever was pleased and laughing about it would ask, "Where's Linda Joy now?" And I would feel obligated to tell the truth, "She killed herself." It would be like the words had killed her then and there.

I decided I didn't have to answer just because somebody asked the question. From then on I'd just say, "She's in Texas," and let it go at that. Finally I stopped telling the story in any form.

But the story hovered. Like a ghost of itself. Like a remembering that back of the story was Linda Joy, real and alive, and waiting. Like Art.

So here it is. For Linda Joy.

*

M

Maggie Magee

There was a time when my worries had me overwhelmed. At night I'd lie awake in bed, thoughts running in my head like tape loops, manic and insistent; no matter how late it was when I called it quits, no matter whether the light was on or off.

I would smoke a third of a joint and read trash until my mind went dead and let me sleep. I'd wake at three in the morning, crying, smoke a third of a joint and read trash until I could sleep. I'd wake in the morning, crying, smoke the final third of the joint, wait to feel deadened out enough to make it seem negligible when I got out of bed, padded like a convalescent to the kitchen to start water for a pot of tea.

As a way to ease the pain it had drawbacks. I was stoned all the time. It made simple things like doing the dishes loom large.

This is all by way of being a preamble.

One evening, driving home from San Francisco to Marin, I realized that I had nothing at home to read myself to sleep with. I pulled into a 7-11 and bought an *Ellery Queen Mystery Magazine;* my memory was that they usually had a "classic" story along with newer writing.

This time they didn't. I read the whole magazine like eating an unsatisfying candy bar. And couldn't sleep.

Okay. If I had to lie awake . . . I started thinking about what a mystery story *should* be, and started thinking about Stanislavsky. Stanislavsky had such muscular control, so they say, that he could flick a muscle to dislodge a fly like horses do. Stanislavsky, when he was going to play the part of an old man, would go to the park, watch old men walk, and see what muscles were inhibited, then he would inhibit those muscles in himself and — here's the point — walk *as well as he could.*

It seemed to me that the hidden factor in a mystery story shouldn't be hidden, the issue was to have a *torque,* a place where the thing twisted, to build that in and then to write the story through like a straight line. I couldn't think of a complex plot but thought of letting a person be the torque, letting one person know two lots of information and having him be the twister.

I got out of bed, got a notebook and wrote a story I called *Max the Mooch*. It let me get to sleep. The next morning I typed it up, naming myself Maggie Magee; when I went to the post office I mailed it off to Ellery Queen and added my phony name to my mailbox list.

Two weeks later Maggie had a letter which included a contract and said if she signed it and sent it back they'd send her seventy-five dollars. I signed it and sent it back.

In another two weeks the check came. I endorsed it as Maggie Magee, then I endorsed it as myself and I deposited it.

The following June, Maggie got two author's copies of the magazine. The name of the story had been changed to *The Man in the Middle*.

In July Maggie was invited to join *Mystery Writers of America*. And she had a letter from the London office of South African Broadcasting wanting to buy the story, to make it into a half-hour radio drama. She signed the SFB contract, adding that she wanted a tape of the show, and mailed it back.

At a time when my own life was a mess my alter-ego was enjoying a success. Her mail was more interesting than mine and she was getting more of it.

I thought, briefly, that I had found a job skill for myself. I wrote another story, typed it, mailed it. It was returned with a standard rejection slip and I never tried another.

*

The Man In The Middle
by Maggie Magee

(from *Ellery Queen Mystery Magazine*, July 1975)

Max was onto something; his nose practically twitched with it, the smell of big money.

What he had were two separate pieces of information. Two independent actions were on the verge of happening, and Max was in the middle.

On the one hand there was Blueboy Sykes, trapped in his second-floor room on Pharaoh Street. Blueboy was a mobster who'd made a couple of mistakes too many. It was a toss-up now who would get him first, the cops or his business associates. He was sitting on an arsenal in his room, with groceries enough for a couple of weeks and his girlfriend to keep him company.

Max had already collected his bit on that piece of information. Because of Max, the cops were staked out on both ends of the street, ready to move in.

Max was a stool pigeon; being a stoolie was his part-time occupation. So he had his thirty pieces of silver from the cops and he had his sixty pieces of silver from the mob. That was just business as usual. Max wasn't interested in the fireworks or the outcome.

On the other hand, and this was more complicated, during the past month there had been some wheeling and dealing over a lookout for a bank job. The first guy Caddie Little had picked had a girlfriend who was determined to make him into a suburban husband. He turned down Caddie's offer and Caddie moved down the list to the next name. The guy who was passed over was trustworthy enough to keep his mouth shut or he wouldn't have been considered in the first place. But his girlfriend was so relieved that she told the story to somebody who told it to somebody who told it to Max.

If you can figure a rat living the lifestyle of a spider, you've got Max. He dealt in threads, connecting this one here and that one there until he had the whole net, or enough to move on; and then he moved.

Down at police headquarters they had him tagged as Maximilian Verga, with a string of numbers under his full-face and profile shots. As a rule his crimes were social: blackmail, extortion, confidence games, though it's hard to imagine he could con anybody with that face. Anyway, between his scams and his arrangements with the cops, he had everybody coming and going. A little hustle here, an armtwist there, a knowledgeable threat somewhere else; it all added up.

And Max was a worker, a full-time walking piece of bad news. It was impossible to imagine Max as anything other than the tenacious rat he had become, hard to think of a little Maxie who was the apple of somebody's eye.

Okay, so that's our hero. The man in the middle. Max marks the spot.

So, a month ago he had got his first inkling of a bank job in the works and had stored it in his memory. The next thing was, Happy Jack Jackson stopped going to the pool hall. To anybody who knew Jack, that meant only one thing—he was working.

Happy Jack was a concentrator. He was either busy being the best pool player in the bars where he hung out or he was nowhere to be seen. Then the holdup of a bank or an armored car would hit the news and Happy Jack would resurface.

It went on like that. Meanwhile, Max fingered Blueboy Sykes.

The next thread was Dee-Dee Wakuski going on a week's vacation from the Peacock Club where she was the featured singer. That meant Dan Moynihan was riding shotgun for the operation. Dee-Dee had an unfortunate tendency to lush a little, just enough to keep her at home whenever Dan was on a job.

That gave Max the lineup of the heavies: Caddie was the brains and backer, Happy Jack was the front man, Dan was the gunner. Max assimilated all that without thinking he'd have an "in." He just automatically sorted and stored it.

Then came his big break.

Max saw Nunzio Sidora leaning against a building and having his shoes shined while he pretended to read a newspaper. Nunzio just happened to be far out of his usual territory and just happened to be across the street from the First National Bank that held down the corner of Main and Pharaoh.

Max was walking along as bravely as his natural slink would let him when he sighted Nunzio. He made an instinctive wheel into the nearest greasy-spoon restaurant and sat back far enough from the plate glass so that he wouldn't be seen. He watched Nunzio get his second shoe polished. Then he watched Nunzio get his first shoe polished again.

Now Nunzio was a reasonable dresser, but he wasn't such a dandy that he'd get a second shoeshine before he'd walked around a little on the first one.

Across the street an armored car pulled up in front of the bank. Nunzio looked up almost casually, glanced at his watch, and read his newspaper. The money bags were carried into the bank, other bags were brought out, and the armored car drove off. Nunzio checked his watch again, folded his newspaper, gave the shoeshine boy a half dollar and walked off down the street.

When he had disappeared Max crossed the street to have his crummy shoes shined.

"That's an absentminded guy," he said to the boy. "He didn't even notice that you shined one of his shoes twice."

"Some kind of a kook," the boy agreed, not looking up from his work. "He's been here three days in a row now."

Now Max had the job pinpointed. He had the bank, the cast; he nearly had the day. Dee-Dee was being advertised to return to the Peacock Club on the coming Saturday night.

Max's second shoe was being shined when he saw a man he knew was a plainclothes dick go into a building across the street. Almost immediately a different dick came out and walked briskly away.

Stakeout, Max thought, and his brain went into a spin. He remembered Blueboy Sykes. All he'd had to do for his money had been pass along an address. Now he was half a block away and hadn't thought twice about it.

What a joke. Nunzio Sidora was casing a bank in a neighborhood where the cops were as busy as alligators in a Tarzan movie.

Max felt his heart go like a trip-hammer. There was something for him in this, he was sure of it. He needed to think. He headed home to his grubby room, locked the door behind him and sat hunched in the gloom, figuring the action.

The main point was, Caddie didn't know he was working into a staked-out neighborhood. But more than that, Max was a key. Max could hurry the cops up. He could give them a story that would cause them to go for Blueboy without further hanging around. Max could guarantee a clear field for Caddie's operation.

And if Caddie didn't come across with a significant amount of money, say a couple of grand, then Max could see he got a police reception the like of which no mayor ever had got. Caddie would have to call the job off unless he had Max's help. And Caddie was already into it for a packet.

Max grinned the nasty grin he saved for when he had somebody by the scruff of the neck.

It would be a little tricky. Caddie was one of the Big Bosses; but Max was on top of it. Max was the guy that could blow the whistle on a Big Boss, for now he was bigger than Caddie.

He licked his lips, picked up the phone and dialed Caddie's Pizza Parlor. They did make pizzas there, terrible ones, for the suckers who didn't know it was a front.

It took a while to get through to Caddie.

"I've got some information you need," Max croaked when Caddie finally was on the other end of the line.

"Max, you got nothing I need," Caddie answered.

"This information you need," Max emphasized. "It's about how healthy the air is around Main and Pharaoh."

He could hear Caddie breathing.

Then, "I'll be free in an hour. I'll expect to see you." Caddie hung up.

Max held the dead receiver, listening to the dial tone turn into a busy signal. He was sweating all over. He was shaking with a chill. He was out of his league and scared. He slowly hung up the telephone. It was a while before his hand stopped shaking.

After a few minutes spent counting his strong points, he felt more secure.

At 5:15 Max was sitting in a room with Caddie Little and two of his boys. The "boys" both cleared six feet by inches and each weighed over 200 pounds. Each had a heavy bulge near his left armpit. "I'm the only one that can get the cops to spring the trap and clear out. Then it'll be a setup for you."

Caddie had sat silent through Max's story.

"You gotta be getting weak in the head, Max. You need some money and you decide I'm the guy that'll pay for a story?" He looked at Max like he was a piece of trash the wind had blown in. "When I need a story I go down the block and pay a couple of bucks at the movie house."

"You'd *know* it was the truth, Caddie! When they get Blueboy Sykes it'll be in the papers. You'll see then it was the truth! I wouldn't try to hand you a line, Caddie." Max's knees felt like mush. Caddie looked at him with eyes as cold as any snake looking at any rat.

"Okay, Willie, give him some money."

Max counted the bills he had been handed.

"There's only five C's here!" he whined.

"Consider yourself lucky, Max," Caddie said. "If it goes all right, I might give you more. If it doesn't go right, I know where to find you."

Max left Caddie's Pizza Parlor with the feeling of cold steel between his shoulder blades.

"That little creep," the hood who had handed him the money exploded.

"No problem," Caddie said softly. "No problem."

When Max got back to his room he called his connection at police headquarters.

"Blueboy's had some money delivered to him and he's set to blow," he said. "How much is that worth?"

The amount was paltry.

Max called Caddie.

"It's all straight, Caddie."

The hood must have been in the phone booth on the corner, waiting for Caddie's call. He was at Max's door within minutes of Max hanging up the telephone.

"Caddie sent you a bonus," he said when Max opened the door.

Max hit the floor, shot twice.

The silencer on the gun was effective. Max laid in a pool of blood while his murderer snooped around for the payoff. There was some extra money with it that got put into a different pocket.

The next morning Blueboy was killed and his girlfriend was wounded in the shootout.

Caddie read the newspaper account with no feelings of gratitude or remorse.

So he was right, Caddie thought, the little creep.

Two days later the bank robbers came out of the bank carrying the canvas bags of money and drove into a cordon of police cars surrounding the area.

Max was the kind of guy who could never resist parlaying his luck. If the sum he could expect for Blueboy was paltry the sum he could expect as a "reward" from the bank was not.

That night half a dozen big guys, including Caddie Little were locked up.

Max was found by his landlady when the smell couldn't be ignored.

Down at headquarters the police clerk who was changing Max's category from Informer to Unsolved Homicide joked that Max had done Society a good turn over his dead body.

*

You can see that I used the phoney lingo we all "know" from the movies and trash books.

I was curious to see what the South Africans did with it. Sure enough, all the South African actors were talking out of the sides of their mouths and through their noses to approximate it, that pseudo reality.

The tape starts with a great crash of symphonic sound that fades under a voice put through massive echo-effects saying, "AND NOW, *the finger of fate!*" And the music swells up again, then down again for, "IN EVERY MAN'S LIFE THERE COMES A TIME WHEN . . ." Well, you can imagine—by this time I had every man being vigorously "GOOSED BY THE FINGER OF FATE," and that isn't what the Announcer said. If I can find that damned tape before this goes to press I'll tell you what more prosaic thing was said.

Then, the question was, how could they deal with it that a *narrator* had described the sequence that now they must express using only dialogue. The answer was, they did it so badly that it sounded more like a stand-up-comic routine.

For starters a guy is saying to the "Chief": "Who da ya tink dis stiff is?"

"How should I know? Pull back de tarp and gimme a gander at his puss, then maybe I can tell you sumpn."

The implication here was that they don't know whose corpse this was, right? Despite the body being that of a man who had been killed in his own bedroom, with the police having been notified by his landlady.

The sheet was pulled off the stiff's puss and the Chief said: "Well, as I live and breathe, it's Maxie Verga. You ever hear about Maxie Verga?"

"Naw, Chief, I never heard of him. Who was he?"

"Just a stoolie. You figure a rat living a lifestyle of a spider you've got Maxie. He's the guy that fingered Caddie Little's bank job. Say . . . I'll bet that had somethin' to do with his gettin' killed. Ya know, I think it must have happened this way . . . "

And with that the Chief becomes omniscient to the point of mind-reading, weather-prophesying, yodeling fantasy.

Well, I enjoyed listening to it.

One time.

Some things, if you do them more than once, you're a pervert.

*

MIDDLE-AGED MIDDLE-CLASS WHITE WOMAN'S STARDUST RAP

I just started noticing all this DUB and RAP stuff and I just thought, 'My God that sounds like back home at the table when nobody'll shut up and *I can do that.*'

In my ongoing program of flashing in the world as a middle-age white woman, I've learned that if I *can* do it, I'd *better.*

I have to warn you that the whole genre must be on its way out because, in the big trickle-down of who notices what when, by the time it gets to me, it's like chili dogs and root beer at the drive-in.

So I had a closer look and there's all this *stuff,* all this machinery, that makes you look and sound better than you are, so my shopping lists are reading . . . Eggs . . . Milk . . . Bread . . . Pitch Transposer . . . Doughnuts . . . Croissants . . . Vocoder . . . and a Casio Sampler if I can afford it after I've paid for my groceries.

So then I need a rhythm ... and I think "What the hell, "Stardust" has always been a showstopper." That was always the last dance just before the last dance ... the last dance was usually "Good Night, Ladies" or "Good Night, Sweetheart" so "Stardust" was always meaningful. They'd drop the lights and start

CHA BOOM/CHA BOOM/CHA BOOM/CHA BOOM BOOM BOOM
CHA BOOM/CHA BOOM/CHA BOOM/CHA BOOM/CHA BOOM
"And now the purple dusk of twilight time,
Steals across the meadows of my heart ... "

*

Misery

Misery doesn't love company.

Misery hovers in bedrooms with doors closed and hates the sound of normal voices elsewhere in the house. Company infringes on misery's righteousness. It's company's fault that I'm breathing wrong.

*

Quotes: M

MARRIAGE

"It is so far from being natural for a man and woman to live in a state of marriage that we find all the motives which they have for remaining in that connection, and the restraints which civilized society imposes to prevent separation, are hardly sufficient to keep them together."

—SAMUEL JOHNSON

*

MONEY
"There are few sorrows, however poignant, in which a good income is of no avail."

—LOGAN PEARSALL SMITH

*

MORON
See the happy moron,
He doesn't give a damn.
I wish I were a moron.
My God! Perhaps I am!

(Eugenics Review, July 1929)

N

Nietzsche's Sister, Elizabeth

. . . married Bernhard Forster, a vigorously active anti-Semite, whom her brother hated. The couple moved to Paraguay where they founded a colony they called "Nueva Germania." Elizabeth's husband killed himself in the middle of a financial scandal. Elizabeth did her best to clean up the mess, tried to keep the colony going and poured unavailing energy into, somehow, turning her deceased husband into a national hero. None of it worked. Disgruntled and disappointed, she returned home to where, unhappily for him but an extraordinary stroke of luck for her, her brother was simultaneously becoming famous and living out the final eleven years of his life in a madhouse.

Friedrich Wilhelm Nietzsche's physical health had been ruined during his service in the Franco-Prussian War. His military service left him half-blind, subject to migraine headaches, and often in physical pain. His writings dealt largely with the need to overcome "the thousandfold impotence" of being. He proposed as the ideal that person who could overcome the problems inherent in his own being.

He felt that when a man or a woman failed in this enterprise of the spirit and became resigned in this failure another, more crude, kind of power often manifested itself—the desire for power over others. "For one thing is needful:" he wrote, "that a human being attain his satisfaction with himself . . . Whoever is disatisfied with himself is always ready to avenge himself therefor; we others will be his victims."

Enter Elizabeth, as if he had conjured up his own personal nightmare, the proof of his insistence.

Elizabeth found herself with a whole new territory. She had control of her brother's papers and began to manipulate them to her own aggrandizement. She became a "writer." She suppressed what she didn't like in her brother's notebooks, tearing out pages and erasing text, and published large excerpts as her own work in a three-volume biography.

It was Elizabeth who courted Hitler, who corrupted Nietzsche's sense of the superior being into a goose-stepping Nazi.

Anyone reading Nietzsche after Elizabeth's use of him has been plagued by her misrepresentation.

But if Nietzsche anticipated his sister's "condition" in the quote made above we can see that he had a hope larger than all that. He believed in the huge circle of eternity, that all things recur in gigantic intervals. The triumph of his own spirit is that, despite that stupid manipulation, his words hold on the page, the words of his "self-overcoming":

"And this slow spider, which crawls in the moonlight, and this moonlight itself, and I and you in the gateway . . . must not all of us have been there before? And return . . . must we not eternally return?"

* O *

Optimism, Ongoing But Intermittent

I keep wandering around in this latest chaos with a feeling of having achieved something.

It's not to be trusted; that's the problem with feelings. I'm addicted to feelings. I particularly like the good ones. And achievement ranks high in my list of desirable attributes. So, for all I know, my feelings have just switched themselves into a self-gratification mode. The part of me that won't trust it is either the inherent Puritan or the informed Cynic.

But... I do have this feeling, like a letter is waiting for me in my mailbox that's an hour away. This time of day, 4:30 P.M., make that two hours if I were to seriously think of getting my car out of this weird place it's parked in and making my way across the Golden Gate Bridge.

Oh, you just wait and see hums sweetly in my head. My optimism can even take my refusals in its stride.

*

Madame Ouspenskaya And The Wolfman

One of the great Russian actresses who left Russia and came to the United States was Madame Maria Ouspenskaya.

She supported herself by teaching Dramatics and by taking the few roles that suited her accent.

She was the grandmother in the Wolfman movies. She sat on the bench seat of the gypsy caravan with its little lantern hanging at the corner and drove the horse so Lon Chaney, Jr., would be free to look up and see that the moon was full. Whenever he looked up, there it was, full and round, with dark nighttime clouds scudding past so the moon looked like it was sailing through the sky at a fast clip. It gave a brilliant light and let us see Lon Chaney, Jr.'s hands growing hair and starting to shape into claws. We saw his face, beginning its transformation, and we saw Madame Ouspenskaya's face, overcome by mingled distress and compassion.

When her grandson was on the verge of being more the wolf than the man, he would leap awkwardly into the road and go running into the dark woods. Madame Ouspenskaya's voice, tender and elegant, would follow him, "Don't go! Stay with me! We will go to the mountains and I will take care of you. You will be *cured!*"

He never stayed. It was always too late. The bright white moon, the grandmother's voice, and the sound of the Wolfman crashing his way through the brush always happened.

I accepted it as I accepted it that when Tarzan grabbed the next vine it always carried him in his intended continuing direction, but somewhere in my depths I noticed. Years went by and all at once, POP, the bubble surfaced.

Why were they always *surprised* by the *full moon?* Even if calendars hadn't been invented, or gypsies didn't use them, they *must* have noticed it sometime, that the moon regularly waxed and waned!

So I began to think about the writer who wrote those movies, and I've figured out what was going on there.

Pre-Menstrual Syndrome Envy.

That writer had a mother or a sister or a girlfriend or a wife or all four, who once a month would scream,

WHAT DO YOU MEAN, GOOD MORNING?

YOU WANT THE CAR KEYS?

THERE IS NO CAR! YOU THINK BECAUSE THERE WAS A CAR YESTERDAY, THERE'S A CAR TODAY! TYPICAL!

(The telephone rings. She rips it out of the wall.)

– 114 –

And he goes to work to write a nice little movie about gypsies, a simple musical romance with violins, with a suitable role for the latest blond starlet who's sleeping with somebody important.

Life is bitter in his mouth. Gypsy violins. An old grandmother. Gypsy girls in low-necked blouses. And Lon Chaney, Jr.

The only role that ever brought out Lon Chaney, Jr.'s talent was when he played a mentally defective hired-hand in *Of Mice and Men*. He fondled small animals to death and carried the corpses around in his pockets until his friend and keeper made him throw them away. The pair dreamed of owning a farm where Lon Chaney, Jr., could take care of the rabbits.

Let's not examine that too closely.

The writer has been pounding his head against the wall trying to think of something he can have Lon Chaney, Jr. *do in gypsy drag. He can't play the violin. He can't dance gypsy dances.*

This is what the writer's life has come to. He's stuck between his job, where he's writing romance for a thirty-five-year-old man with a hoop in his ear whose grandmother won't let him drive the wagon, and his home, where he's regularly got a madwoman with monthly perks, and he can't blame her because she doesn't *do* it. It *happens* to her.

And *voilà!*

The full moon crashes in the sky like a gong and Lon Chaney, Jr., grows teeth and claws and kills everything in sight.

Madame Ouspenskaya will never take him to the mountains in time.

He will never be cured.

He is helpless forever under the transforming moon.

P

Quotes: P

Printing

"In a certain sense, printing proved a drawback to letters. It
... cast contempt on books that failed to find a publisher."
—REMY DE GOURMONT

*

Q

Dale Herd's Found Quarter

Dale Herd telephoned me.

"I was just walking down the street and I found a quarter on the sidewalk."

"Good for you."

"Then when I went to pick it up it was epoxied to the cement."

"Hell."

"What I really hated about it was I knew the son-of-a-bitch was somewhere watching me. So I went looking for a good rock and I came back and I knocked the quarter off the sidewalk."

"Spoiled his game."

"Yeah, it would cost him another quarter to keep it up. So then I had this quarter and I wanted to do something with it and I decided to telephone you with it and tell you."

"I'm glad I was home."

*

Queen Victoria and Quote

A middle-aged British matron at a performance of *Cleopatra* by Sarah Bernhardt is supposed to have said, "How different, how very different from the home life of our own dear Queen!"

*

R

Raisins

There is a kind of pleading eye that, instead of melting, inviting sympathy, has gone opaque. It is the eye of the person who is conditioned to being too demanding, to being too often resisted. The eye goes blank to not notice, to let itself continue. It is the eye of mothers who offer what their child has no interest in.

The child, myself, a child more than fifty years old, seeing that eye, that blanking out of my resistance to yet another unwanted generosity, must feel myself ungenerous at again refusing what is offered. Once again I am not wanting an entire wardrobe in polyester despite You Can Just Throw It in the Washing Machine. Once again I feel guilty at refusing the offer, and at the cringing way I circle the offer, and I feel guilty at that opaque eye, surely the result of my accrued refusals. I even feel guilty at noticing the eyes as if I have an overview of the event, and on and on.

In this instance it was raisins.

"... I've tried eating some of them but they just upset my stomach, but I don't think that means they've gone bad. Why don't you have some of them, if you're hungry for something sweet."

It's a double availability—the raisins are not only there but I'm their last chance. It's a salvaging.

That's much more benign than my ex-husband who would say, "God, this is really awful—taste it," and then feel angered and cheated if I insisted on taking his word for it. He hated it that he had had the rotten experience of tasting something bad while I apparently lived a life of milk and honey. In the last years of that marriage, he was convinced that I was being treated unfairly by the world, better than I deserved to be treated.

And here it is again. He's bitten into something foul and I haven't.

*

Quotes: R

REVIEW OF LADY CHATTERLEY'S LOVER

"Although written many years ago, *Lady Chatterley's Lover* has just been reissued by the Grove Press, and this pictorial account of the day by day life of an English gamekeeper is full of considerable interest to outdoor-minded readers as it contains many passages on pheasant-raising, the apprehending of poachers, ways to control vermin and other chores and duties of the professional gamekeeper.

"Unfortunately one is obliged to wade through many pages of extraneous material in order to discover and savor those sidelights on the management of a Midland shooting estate, and in this reviewer's opinion the book cannot take the place of J. R. Miller's *Practical Gamekeeping.*"

—ED ZERN
Field and Stream Magazine, 1959

*

S

Silver Shoes

People who live alone do what they want to do any time of the day or night. Without thought for anyone else, particularly not for persons who might disapprove and therefore stop them.

So thought she who took the orange box down from a shelf in the closet, late at night, and put on her new shoes. They were lightweight loafers, shiny silver. They had cost her $5.00, on sale, marked down from $21.95.

It was a hot night, the last of July, and she was visiting her mother but would leave in three days. She was lying on cotton-and-polyester sheets printed blue and green and pink plaid. Except for the shoes she was completely naked. Lying and reading a book, she remembered the shoes she had bought two days earlier. She put them on, thinking she couldn't have done it if she had still been with the husband she had been married to for twenty-four years, who had married a woman who was twenty-seven.

He would have had attitudes about it, including the attitude that anything he thought about anything she did mattered as much as anything she thought about it. To be truthful, he would have believed that what he thought about her actions mattered more than what she thought about them. Unfair, but that wasn't quite the word, more than unfair it was untrue. She continued to be puzzled about it, that he had believed himself to be so inherently pre-emptive. It had confused and distressed her when they were together. Now that they weren't together it puzzled her when she thought about it, as now. She would never resolve it in her mind.

But now, living alone, and all that adjusting gone through and done with, she thought it might be ideal to not be growing old alongside a man who would have had attitudes about it whenever it caught his eye. It was better to be alone, and naked, on a bed late at night, in silver shoes.

*

Spouses Of Writers

Chamfort said, "Diderot used to say that a writer may have a mistress who fashions books, but must have a wife who fashions shirts."

I could come up with endless variations on the theme of what a writer's husband should be.

*

* T *

A Thousand Pieces

"I'm looking for an eye. I need a blue left eye. And if the piece is big there may be some hair there, blond hair."

"He always said he adored her and that he wanted to make her happy. That's how men are, at first. And she believed him, that's how she is."

"This brown-and-blue bit with two things sticking out and one sticking in, Anna, does it go over . . ."

"Great! I probably looked right over it a dozen times."

"She's got 'happy' stuck in her head. She looked awful after they pumped out her stomach. I asked her how she felt, which has to be the most goddamned stupid . . . What else can you say? I'd already said hello. It was time to say something else. I couldn't say there's a sale at Macy's or how's your new car running, so I said 'How are you feeling?' And she said 'Jimbo is going to be so mad.'"

"Here's a piece of your tree."

"Look at that! No wonder I couldn't figure it out. They've cut right through that little white flower; that means I need a tiny blob of white and all the rest blue."

"You've got my eye stuck in that underbrush, Jean. You must've jammed it in."

"I *wondered* what that thing was. I didn't jam it. It's one of those pieces they duplicate the shape of to fool you."

"I asked her, 'If all Jimbo wants is to make you happy how come you're so miserable?' and she said she's always been inclined to misery."

"That's not true."

"That's what I told her. Jimbo came in all upset and the nurse told us we had to leave the room for a minute while she did something or other, and out in the hall Jimbo thought I should give him some kind of sympathy. You know that hangdog poor-old-me look he gets. All I did was talk about Cissy. I said it was a good thing they found her in time. So then he says, 'Margaret, what can I do to help her?' Like it was all her problem and he was trying to understand. I said, 'If you stop getting drunk and coming home and beating her up that would be a beginning.' But he acted like I hadn't opened my mouth."

"It *is* her problem. It won't get solved until she leaves him."

"That's not going to happen. Here's your white-flower-blue-sky piece. And look at this corner on it and this black squiggle . . . that means it fits . . . where's that piece we couldn't figure out?"

"Here! Look, it's a bird!"

"It's a plane! It's Superman!"

"She won't leave him. She's got loyalty like other people have typhoid."

"Nobody has typhoid anymore."

"Remember that red plaid dress she had?"

"Oh, my god, the world's *worst* dress."

"Remember how she hung onto that dress? Remember, we figured out how to get her rid of that dress."

"Jean, I'm about to make your day. Here's *this,* and *this,* and *this!* Now does that or does it not let you fit on that whole long string of greenery you've been hogging?"

"It does! It really does! I think we should put a puzzle together sometime where we count the pieces somebody puts down as points. That way we could have a winner. We could ante a penny for each piece and . . . "

"Oh, shut up."

"The more we told her how awful that dress was the more she wore it."

"She's always been tenderhearted. I'll bet she still has every doll she ever owned."

"I don't remember that dress. It must have been before my time. Here, Margaret, here and here and here."

"Leave something for me to do, if you please."

"Mary, here's the rest of your tiger stripe."

"That's a relief. I hate it when there's a hole. I'm always convinced there's a piece missing."

"None of the pieces are missing."

"What happened about the dress? Did it get worn out?"

"Naw. It was made out of nylon and steel, something indestructible. We started bragging on it. Whenever she wasn't wearing it we'd ask her why not. We started acting like it was the only dress she had that we liked."

"Margaret said we had to make her think that dress didn't need her to protect it. So after a while she passed it on to the Salvation Army like she was being Lady Bountiful to some total stranger."

"Here, Jean, this looks like you."

"Yeah. It's going fast now. You get down to the last third and it gets easy."

"There's no way to brag up Jimbo."

"We *used* to like him. We *used* to think he had some gifts. What were they?"

"They were mostly how happy he made Cissy."

"He's a good mechanic. He keeps their cars going."

"He used to be better-looking. When he was thinner. Before he ate so much of Cissy's cooking."

"Overlook the paunch. Tell her how good he looks."

"And when he does one of those paltry things he does in front of people to make himself look good act like it proves he's a dream walking."

"I don't think I should get in on this. I don't think I can keep a straight face."

"When you feel like laughing just think of how Cissy looked two days ago when we brought her home from the hospital."

"She *knows* how we feel about Jimbo. She won't believe us for a minute."

"Yes, she will. She'll believe us in the exact same place where she believes that Jimbo wants her to be happy. We're applying ointment straight to the damage."

"She *knew* that red dress was awful. She just couldn't stand being the one that doomed it."

"What if she really loves him?"

"She does really love him. The problem is still how she can leave him. Every time we tell her she has to leave him she gets sorry for how he's going to be without her. She's got to be able to tell herself that he has other options open."

"Doesn't she count that woman in his office and that one he took to Las Vegas as him having options?"

"It's got turned into 'Jimbo goes out with other women because she's not keeping him satisfied at home.'"

"God, I remember *that* one!"

"Well, I'm willing to try if all of us try. I sure don't want to show up on the scene talking about how great Jimbo is unless you all do it too."

"He'd think you were making a pass at him."

"That's his style. He's going to think we're all hot for his body."

"There's bound to be a little confusion at first. Let's only go in pairs so we won't get left alone in a room with him."

"How about Cissy?"

"I think she'll guess, but I think she'll blank it."

"It's cynical to think that good-hearted people are just wearing blinkers."

"Blinkers?"

"Blinders."

"Blinders?"

"You know, those things they used to put on horses to keep them from being distracted."

"I'm too young for that."

"Hah!"

"Anybody got any use for this weird shape?"

"I've been looking for something sort of like that. Only . . . that's it . . . it goes in *this* way."

"There now."

"Boy, this is a *dull* picture! All that work to end up with *this?*"

"That's not the point."

*

Tomahto

The young Englishwoman who never got the point sang, in a high sweet voice, "You say tomahto and I say tomahto. You say potahto and I say potahto. Tomahto. Tomahto. Potahto. Potahto. Let's call the whole thing off."

*

Travel

I'm on a plane where everyone is wearing name tags.

"I passed up China!" a woman says, and then insists, "I'll go *anywhere!* I'll go *anywhere!*"

"So will my daughter," says the woman she's talking to, who asks, "Philadelphia?"

– 131 –

No, the woman who passed up China has never been to Philadelphia but would if she could is the implication, though the lustre in her voice fades slightly.

She'll never say to a stranger, "I've just come from *Philadelphia!*" as she said to this one, "I've just come from *New Zealand!*"

Within the variorum of "anywhere" there are "wheres" that matter more.

Through the window at my side I watch the ground rise like water to fill the glass.

*

Things

The thought of unpacking my "things" and sitting in the middle of them curdles my soul. Apparently I'm making other choices. If only choices were solutions . . . Over-the-falls is my style, a choice that precludes most others. Over-the-falls feels like hope to me. I am waiting for a miracle. A miracle is whatever might happen to resolve all this. I've cleared the slate. I'm ready.

*

Quotes: T

"She was not quite what you would call refined. She was not quite what you would call unrefined. She was the kind of person that keeps a parrot."

—MARK TWAIN

*

U

Uncertainty Principle

Formulated by Heisenberg in 1927, the Uncertainty Principle states that it is impossible to simultaneously determine the location and the velocity of a body in motion with full accuracy. The more particularly the one is addressed, the more insecure becomes the other.

The Encyclopedia Britannica says that this uncertainty is of no consequence in much ordinary experience.

The two places where it matters are in atomic experiments and in philosophy.

The Britannica ends its discussion — more than a full page and with a great chunk of bibliography — by sandwiching a wonderful diatribe against the principle (P.W. Bridgman, *Harper's Magazine*, 1929) between two antiacid nonstatements.

In a sense it is meaningless to argue which view is correct, since inherently unobservable natural properties defy objective evaluation. In this connection it is well to quote P.W. Bridgman:

The immediate effect [of the uncertainty principle] will be to let loose a veritable intellectual spree of licentious and debauched thinking. This will come from the refusal to take at its true value the statement that it is meaningless to penetrate much deeper than the electron, and will have the thesis that there is really a domain beyond, only that man with his present limitations is not fitted to enter this domain. . . . The existence of such a domain will be made the basis of an orgy of rationalizing. It will be made the substance of the soul . . . the principle of vital processes will have its seat here; and it will be the medium of telepathic communication. One group will find in the failure of the physical law of cause and effect the solution of the age-old problem of the freedom of the will, and, on the other hand, the other hand, the atheist will find the justification of his contention that chance rules the universe.

The least arguable conclusion is that man should remain humble in the face of nature since there are inherent limitations to the precision with which he can observe.

(And, while we're about it, let's do cling with a decent, however desperate, tenacity, to whatever sense of humor we can manage.)

*

Quotes: U

Unknowns (Statements By)

"Experience teaches you to recognize a mistake when you've made it again."

"Time is nature's way of keeping everything from happening at once."

"A closed mouth gathers no feet."

"Bagpipes are a joke the Irish played on the Scots, and the Scots didn't get it."

"In every fat book there is a thin book trying to get out."

"Life is extinct on other planets because their scientists were more advanced than ours."

"Only dead fish go with the flow."

"I will always cherish the initial misconceptions I had about you."

*

* V *

Voyages Of Discovery

The 110-year-old black man, dressed up in a suit and tie and a felt hat, stood there on a field in Texas (July 21, 1969) waiting, like everybody else, for a man to step onto the moon. We were watching it on a television set in Gloucester, Massachusetts. Bob's German translator was part of an international project at Harvard for the summer and had come to visit, bringing a Swiss, an Austrian, a Frenchman, a Dutch woman.

We all sat like an impromptu League of Nations, watching the television screen where the astronauts kept not doing it. The image we were shown kept going between the real astronauts and a studio mock-up. It was hard to know when we were seeing the real thing and when they were filling in with their own invention. At intervals they'd shift to the black man in his hat and talk to him about slavery, or list the things that had happened during his lifetime, just about everything significant that had happened to the "civilized" world. It seemed that all he'd missed was the Voyages of Discovery, but he was making up for it now. He hadn't been there when Columbus stepped onto the New World but some P.R. executive had rounded him up to be here for this next one, this "giant step for mankind." He did his best whenever some announcer stuck a microphone in his face; he smiled and was polite and when he was asked some dumb question he would do his best to answer appropriately.

He agreed with them when they told him that this must be an exciting day for him. "Oh, yes," he said, "this *is* an exciting day," and he smiled. He had a very sweet, very polite smile. The camera switched back to the studio replication.

In the kitchen our cat, Aphrodite, started having kittens. She was one of the most beautiful cats I've ever had, and the most pissed-off. She went through her days glaring. She had a real temperament. In keeping with her misanthropic tendencies, she popped a litter of the most uninteresting kittens I've ever seen. They were mewling, wet, pathetic objects.

The Frenchman and the Dutch woman and Bob's translator, Klaus, were particularly interested and livened the boring business of waiting for the astronaut to step out of the spaceship by walking at intervals into the kitchen to see how many kittens there were now.

It was getting dark in Texas; the camera crew were pleased that they could train their cameras heavenward and show the old moon sailing along, not looking like any new thing was going on.

In the kitchen Aphrodite looked at the kittens in the box as if they were boring invaders. They nuzzled at her belly, latched onto her tits and she watched them.

Finally the ladder going down wasn't a simulation, it was the real ladder, the man coming down it in his space garb was a real man, he took the first real steps in the moon dust and the camera photographed the foot-shaped prints.

In Texas at least three different camera crews confronted the 110-year-old man while an announcer, pointing up, said, "Well, it's happened. How do you feel about it, that right now there's a man walking on the moon?"

And now the old man knew it was true, what he had suspected earlier, that he was in the company of fools. The smile left his face and he said "There ain't no man on the moon!"

"There is! There really is!" the announcer insisted.

"There ain't no man on the moon!" the old man said, very dignified, an absolute quality in his voice. He turned and walked away from all the cameras.

*

Vicious Valentine

Here I sit all broken-hearted
Loved a twit but now we've parted
The present's grim the future's brighter
He shouldn't have done it to a writer

—B.L.H.

*

* W *

Work And Getting On With It

I've sometimes thought of it as a gift hanging in wait in the future, a benefaction that would only be desirable when it came about; *with youth and beauty flown one might now decently get on with the work.*

Vanity stops work getting done. Stanislavsky said that every time he gained one hard-earned step forward he remembered that he looked good in tights and slid back two. We all know people, male and female, who might have achieved something if they hadn't been beautiful.

But vanity is a powerful habit. Everyone, I've read, believes themselves to look ten pounds lighter than they actually are, and ten years younger.

This is all to say that I've just had a photo session and got a part of the result, a pair of pictures that I can have for my "files."

The experience of these pictures is terrifying. The Picture of Dorian Gray, come home to roost.

How could I have become so old and pathetic, a faltering smile on my lips and my eyes lost in the map of an apparently mountainous region, without my having noticed? And I am so caught into my delusion that looking at my face in the bathroom mirror and looking at the photograph I hold adjacent to it still does not convince me. I just can't agree that that . . .

It may simply be a bad photograph. I have a history of photographing strangely, of only finding one acceptable photograph out of a multitude.

But even if that is the case, even if in the thirty pictures the photographer took there lurk a few that look as I think I look, even so, I have taken this picture to heart. That face is mine, if not now, in the not-too-distant future. That face faces the facts and so must I.

I have been a notorious hard case. I only acknowledged that I was middle-aged when I turned fifty. Admittedly, both my grandmothers lived to be nearly a hundred and I expect my mother to do the same but, as we all know, *middle-age* has nothing to do with being midway through one's life, otherwise persons who die young could be it at the age of two or ten or twenty. *Middle-age* is a social description—it puts one in one's place.

Thinking of oneself as young is taken as a vanity but it might more accurately be thought of as a habit, encouraged by years of practice. All those years of being young, with age in abeyance, remote as any accident that happens to others, and even that remove proving itself day after day. So one is naturally deluded by a reality that maintains itself in time—the time that continues to pass—and finds oneself mistaken, inherently wrong, without having done anything other than what one has always done.

Society, quite without malice, begins to correct that error. Clues begin to proliferate. One of the first social symptoms of aging is that other people get decent about it. They evade the subject, or they begin to tell you, more often than you expect to hear it, how well you are looking.

You might be told that you've become a 'role model.'

Terrifying.

I'm still hoping to be past my confusions, still hoping to get my skills together, and here is someone suggesting that I am a completed item, caught to all these imperfections, saying they think to fashion themselves on me. Low standards, I call it.

So, there I was, having opened the envelope with some pleasurable anticipation. My memory was that I had looked okay that day the pictures were taken. And then there I was with my own face in my hand, the face of the dreadful truth. The time had come to shift and reorganize great chunks of my thought and assumption if I meant to not become *a silly old woman.*

There are these other leavings and habits from our youth. We made judgments about older people. We disliked *silliness* in them, and *self-centeredness,* and mistaken notions of themselves as *young* and *attractive* and *forceful.* And we assumed they were those things through a lack of capacity. They were incapable of making these distinctions and hadn't, therefore, the ability to change them.

Whereas we, seeing so clearly, meant to be quite different.

And that righteousness, being unchallenged, glided through the limbo of passing time with us, a passenger, or rather, a guest. A guest who, in my case, has just stepped forward to demand her privileges. More clean towels! A change of sheets! No silliness! And will I please, as we long ago agreed, become an old lady who is still slim, who is elegant, doesn't dye her hair, and does not wear clothes patently intended for young persons. *No more Levi's,* for instance, and *please don't be a blot on the landscape by wearing a bathing suit!*

I feel my hackles rise.

It's quite enough to accept my age and condition. I don't intend to also have the overlay of adolescent self-consciousness that posits myself as perfectible and implies that all the world is watching.

If there is anything that middle-aged women learn it is that they have become slightly invisible.

The photographs: I can accept this photograph as an act of personal edification, but I'm not going to send it out as a self-advertisement, which is one of the things I wanted it for.

I called the woman who had chosen the pictures to ask whether there hadn't been any that made me more *attractive*.

"I thought that picture had such character," she said.

"Character" indeed! I know that inclination to admire ruins so long as one needn't live there.

Of course, there *are* facelifts and tummytucks; men and women in their seventies with back injuries got from weight lifting. But there's also this other thing.

Can I really make the shift into that anticipated advantage, that gift, that *getting on with the work?*

*

Quotes: W

"The test of a book (to a writer) is if it makes a space in which, quite naturally, you can say what you want to say."
— VIRGINIA WOOLF

*

Writing And Blame

"As the faculty of writing has been chiefly a masculine endowment, the reproach of making the world miserable has been always thrown upon the women."
— SAMUEL JOHNSON

*

Writing And Clarity

"Sperone-Speroni explains very well why a writer's form of expression may seem quite clear to [the writer] yet obscure to the reader: the reader is advancing from language to thought, the writer from thought to language."

—CHAMFORT

*

* X *

Quotes: X

"The letters which when made public in 1798 nearly involved France and the United States in war. By orders of the French Directory fully a thousand U.S. vessels had been stopped on the high seas for examination. President Adams sent three commissioners, C. Pinckney, Marshall and Gerry, to France to negotiate a treaty which would do away with this annoyance. The commissioners were met in France by three agents who demanded a large sum of money before the Directory would receive the commission and also notified the commission that France would expect a loan from the United States if satisfaction of any other kind was to be given. The commissioners upon rejecting these overtures were ordered out of France. Their report was published at once in the United States and in it the French agents were labeled X, Y, and Z, from which the correspondence took its name. The United States increased its army and navy, and hostilities were actually begun, when Talleyrand disavowed any connection with the agents and agreed to receive any minister the United States might send."

—*Encyclopedia Britannica*, 14th ed.

*

Y

Quotes: Y

Out-worn heart, in a time out-worn,
Come clear of the nets of wrong and right;
Laugh, heart, again in the grey twilight,
Sigh, heart, again in the dew of the morn.

*

An aged man is but a paltry thing,
A tattered coat upon a stick, unless
Soul claps its hands and sing, and louder sing
For every tatter in its mortal dress.

                          —W. B. YEATS

*

Z

Zayde

Zayde is the chief character in a Romance written by Mme. Lafayette.

It was also the first name of the first woman my first husband took to bed after our marriage. She was a nurse at the hospital in Belize, where I was having our first daughter.

I thought the name was an invention of her mother's, a variation on Sadie, until I saw this other reference and was reminded.

*

Quotes: Z

ZEAL
"The most important thing women have to do is stir up the zeal of women themselves."
> —JOHN STUART MILL
> (letter to Alexander Bain,
> July 14, 1869)

*

ZED
"Thou whoreson zed! thou unnecessary letter!"
> —SHAKESPEARE
> (*King Lear* II.ii)

*